MERCIFUL LIES

JERSEY BAD BOYS
BOOK 1

C.D. GORRI

MERCIFUL LIES

Jersey Bad Boys
Book 1
By C.D. Gorri

Copyright C.D. Gorri, NJ 2024

Before you begin sign up for my newsletter here:
SUBSCRIBE HERE

DEDICATION

If you've always been drawn to the villain's side, rooting for all the Jokers, the Lokis, and the Goblin Kings, stick around. You might like this.

Special thanks to Book Nook Nuts and to my Beta and ARC teams. I can't do any of this without you.
xoxo, C.D.

There's no room for mercy in a kingdom built on lies.

Beneath the veneer of polite society exists a criminal organization known for its utter lack of mercy. They call themselves the Vipers. The men who belong to this syndicate are cruel, cunning, and unforgiving. Ruled by a king, this band of brothers knows no boundaries and takes no prisoners. To cross them is to sign your own death certificate.

But even serpents have weaknesses.

And sometimes that weakness is just a flower.

Our Bad Boys:

Nico Fury

Luc Batiste

Angel Fury

Content Warnings:

This is a contemporary romance series of connected standalones, featuring familiar tropes such as enemies to lovers, forced proximity, arranged marriages, secret babies, and contains some violence, and explicit sex scenes. Profanity, graphic, steamy scenes, violence, homicide, talk of deceased relatives, references to sexual assault and abuse (not by the MCs), mention of domestic violence (not perpetrated by MCs), mention of suicide, alcohol consumption, misogyny (not the MCs), questionable morals, hurtful past, manipulations, fake relationships, lies, revenge, forced marriages, very bad decisions, and romantic obsessions that may be unhealthy, or toxic.

This is a fictional story with fictional characters. This is not real life.

**Always take care of your mental, emotional, and physical self because you are important.*

Lies can be merciful. It just depends on the why.

Anna

I knew the second I saw him, my life would change forever. When my brother offers me as payment to Nico Fury, the king of the Vipers, how can I refuse? Tattooed, built, and tall, he was the only man I saw when I walked into the room. It was like he occupied all the available space, sitting on his throne of blood, sweat, and lies.

Nerves assailed me, but I owed my brother too much to let anything happen to him. One night. That was all. But it would leave me wrecked. Actions always had consequences. Six months later, my brother was killed by a rival organization, and now they were after me.

There was only one place I could go to keep my unborn baby safe. I just hoped the king would be merciful.

Nico

Perfect things didn't exist, at least not in my

experience. But she was pretty close. I had her in my bed for one night, and I couldn't shake the memory.

No, I wasn't meant to keep soft things like Anna Keller. My life belonged to my crew, and we were a vicious group. Hell, we weren't called Vipers for nothing.

But she was different. She made me want, and I loved and hated her for it. Anna was light in a world of constant darkness. She was all warmth and beauty like no other. And I craved her like a drug.

Six months had passed since I took her in return for clearing her brother's debt to me, but that man attracted trouble like honey did flies. It wasn't long before I learned Sam Keller had gotten himself killed. Less than an hour later, Anna came back to me, on her knees, asking for sanctuary.

I knew the moment I saw the swell of her stomach she was carrying my baby. Anna thought coming here would protect her, but she was walking right into the Viper's nest. Before I was finished, my little runaway would be begging me for mercy.

CHAPTER ONE-ANNA

I t's New Year's Eve. I can't believe it.

The last night of another long, boring year where I can't manage to make ends meet and I'm stuck in the same rut as always.

Shit.

I hate feeling this way. The old clock makes a constant ticking noise from where it hangs on the office wall, and I frown at the dingy beige color.

When was the last time we painted?

"Anna, you have payroll? Or are you late again?" Javi asks, walking into my office without knocking.

This guy. Ugh.

I knew it was going to be different after Dad died. But five years have passed and neither of the two crews of bakers working for us treated me with anything even close to respect.

Sammy is supposed to help. He found Javi to run the crews, but with him came a huge bump in their pay and things are worse than ever.

"I told you I got it, Javi. Gimme a second." I look down, counting out the envelopes for his two seven-man crews.

He's the leader, so his cut is bigger, then it's up to him to divvy out cash to his men. He has a second guy who takes care of the other shift.

They are both the newest but have the most clout. The old bakers do as they are told. They were always hard workers and kind.

These guys though, they are not nice. Javi is always asking for more money and he is never satisfied with my efforts to placate him.

Bread is a cash business. Always has been.

That's probably why Dad got into trouble so often with loan sharks and bookies. My brother Sammy takes after him, and I can't help but worry.

I'm nine years older than Sammy. He's twenty-two to my thirty-one, and absolutely no help at all running the family business.

Delilah's Bakery has been around for sixty years. There's no Delilah in my family, but that was the name of the old woman my grandfather, the first Samuel Keller, bought it from fifty years ago.

Me and my brother are the third generation of Kellers to run this thing, and honestly, I'm not sure how much longer I can do it.

"Anna," Javi calls my name again, and I can tell he's getting annoyed.

"Here," I snap, handing him a stack of envelopes. "I'll leave the rest on the desk before I go for the night."

"No problem, Anna. You do that."

He makes me uncomfortable, but I ignore it and I finish what I am doing.

I pack up my purse and shrug into my raggedy winter coat. Christmas came and went, and with it all the good feelings associated with the season.

I hate winter. New Jersey isn't terribly cold yet. But it's gray. And it's wet.

And I wish it was summer.

I wave goodbye to the rest of the bakers as I walk through the storefront and switch off lights, locking the door behind me.

The apartment I rent is a few blocks away, and I hustle through the damp streets, bracing myself for the icy breeze and the rush of people.

"Oops, excuse me. Happy New Year!"

A beautiful half-dressed woman flashes me a brilliant smile as she races to catch the Uber that's double parked

I smile back and shake my head. It's not a big deal that she almost knocked me down.

Actually, it might have been the most exciting thing to happen to me in weeks.

Well, there was that coffee Eric brought me the other day, but that hardly counted.

Eric is a Firefighter who came in to buy French bread for the house every Tuesday.

I'd known him for years and read nothing into it. Eric is just a friendly guy.

I stand there a moment longer than is appropriate, just watching the young woman as she talks animatedly into her phone.

The car pulls away and I feel guilty for wishing we could trade places.

It's New Year's Eve and I have no plans, nowhere to go, and no one to dress up for.

Boring.

My life is so boring.

The sound of Pancake meowing greets me as I push the door open. The bag of dough I took from the bakery bangs against it, and I make cooing noises to my kitty.

Pizza sounds like fun, and I like homemade best. That way I can control the amount of sauce and cheese.

I know it's weird, but I really don't like a lot of greasy cheese on my pizza. In fact, sometimes I just use a little grated pecorino romano and skip the mozz altogether.

"Come here, Pancake. I got something for you."

I pull the package of fresh salmon I picked up for him earlier and grin when he pounces on the countertop

He's the prettiest kitty I ever saw. All golden, just like a pancake, or so Sammy always said.

Sadness slithers into my heart like a serpent ready to strike, and I close my eyes for a moment against the feeling.

I don't want to be sad. New Year's Eve is all about new beginnings, and I truly hope wherever he is, my brother is making a fresh start.

But those hopes die the second I hear pounding on my front door.

Pancake laps at his salmon as I cross the room and pull the door open, undoing my three security locks first.

"Sammy!" I shout, taking in his bloody form.

There's a big, brooding man behind him, heavily muscled and covered in tattoos.

"Anna," my brother rasps, and I walk him to the couch.

"What is going on?"

"Your brother owes some money to my boss. He says you can make good," the behemoth rumbles.

"What? Sammy?" I sputter, trying to get my brother to look at me.

"Did you beat him?" I ask.

"He knows better than to take money from the Vipers," the man says with a cruel twist of his lips.

Oh shit.

The Vipers?

I want to slap my brother across the face for messing around with that group of criminals.

"I'm sorry, Anna. I need h-help. P-please," he begs, dark brown eyes like my father's peer up at me through swollen, broken skin.

My eyes are brown too, but they're lighter. More whiskey than chocolate.

"H-how much does he owe?" I ask the stranger, knowing I will do whatever I can to help.

"Fifty-five," he says.

I blink. Fifty-five dollars? That can't be right. Then it hits me.

Oh my God!

"You owe the Vipers fifty-five thousand dollars!" I shout.

It's not a question. My brother hangs his head, snot and tears rolling down his face as he sobs like the big baby he is.

"Oh, Sammy, why?"

"I'm sorry, Anna. I'm sorry! But you have to help me," he begs, grabbing my shirt.

I gently remove his hands and turn to face the giant. His expression is stony. His mood is unreadable.

"I have seven thousand dollars in my savings account and another three in my checking, I can bring your boss both the day after tomorrow," I tell him, knowing it's a holiday and they won't be open.

"Not good enough, sweetheart. Besides, your baby bro didn't promise the king your money."

"He didn't?"

"No. He promised him you."

CHAPTER TWO-ANNA

Fear slithers down my spine as I walk into the bar known as the Vipers' Den. It's dark and loud, and full of people.

I pause in my procession, my hand clutching my throat.

Damn.

I can't breathe.

"Hey Angel, who's the sacrifice?" a beautiful woman tending bar yells in our direction.

"Just tend the bar, Maria."

His name is Angel. Hers is Maria.

I store the information away, assuming it will be useful someday. She is still staring daggers at me, and I have no idea what I did to offend her.

A large hand pushes between my shoulder blades, propelling me forward, and I continue to move.

"Down the stairs," he growls, nodding at the guy sitting on a stool blocking the entryway.

My assumption is he's some sort of security guard. He's big and muscular, has almost as many tattoos as Angel over here, but really, what do I know?

There's music blasting through speakers, and I'm surprised at how trendy the place is inside. I expected a dive, but it's not that.

The ceilings are exposed, giving it that edgy industrial look, and everything seems made of steel or iron and wood. The vibe is strong, powerful and utterly masculine.

I can hardly hear myself think as the next raunchy song comes on. This one has a heavier bass, and the lead singer is wailing.

I don't know the song. But it's not bad.

My taste in music, like everything else, is eclectic. I listen to everything from classical to classic rock. It all depends on my mood.

But I'm not there for music. I'm there to offer myself like a freaking sacrifice, just like the pretty bartender said. To try to pay my brother's debts with my body.

I just hoped the king, as Angel called him, doesn't mind curvy girls.

I am what I am. I was never skinny. But I am healthy despite being sixty pounds overweight, according to my primary.

It seems like a lie, but it's not. I'm active. I eat right, I just eat a lot, I guess.

But even though I'm a size sixteen, I don't hate my body like society suggests I should. Who has time for all that?

I'm so busy trying to make ends meet it's all I can do to manage a home cooked meal a couple of nights a week. Mostly, I eat at the bakery. Cold cuts and ramen noodles, that kind of thing.

"Keep going."

Angel's gruff voice interrupts my wayward thoughts and I wonder how a man who looks like an actual demon got a name like that.

He's huge. Easily six and a half feet tall, and maybe half as wide. The guy could be a professional football player with those shoulders.

But something tells me he isn't exactly into sportsmanship. Maybe it's the *malocchio*, protection against the evil eye, tattoo on his giant biceps or the snake wrapped around a rose inked across his throat that tells me that.

No, it's his cold blue eyes. They look dead. Like a shark.

Either way, this isn't a guy I want to fuck with.

I hug myself as I walk carefully down the darkened staircase, following the path to an even darker hallway.

I stumble, but the man behind me grabs my elbow and stops me from falling.

"Look, I don't know what your boss expects—"

"He expects to be paid, Anna Keller. One night with you or it's your brother's life. If it ain't worth it to you, I'll take you back," he says, pulling me towards the way we just came.

I dig my heels in, shaking my head. Terror threatens to bring me to my knees. I'm not a femme fatale or a working girl. I don't know how to be sexy or seductive.

But I'll do just about anything for Sammy. I promised Dad on his deathbed that I'd look out for him.

Always. That was my promise.

My brother isn't the easiest person to love.

I was still young by the time both our parents died, but I'm one of those old souls. The kind of person who is born with a sense of responsibility some never seem to feel.

Sammy is one of them. He is selfish and spoiled. I can't think of a single thing he's ever done for anyone else.

Seems like he is always in trouble. He got kicked out of school. Had problems with drugs and drinking. Now, with the gambling, it was like Dad all over again.

But he's still my brother. And I'll do this for him. I'll give myself to a stranger. A man who by all accounts should terrify me.

"Alright then," Angel says.

He's nodding as if he's made his mind up about something.

What? I have no idea.

"There's a door on the left, go in. Get undressed. And wait for the king."

The first time Sam Keller walked into my bar I knew the punk was nothing but trouble.

Young. Cocky. Arrogant. Practically fucking oozing bad luck.

The Vipers are involved in a little of this and a little of that. Most of our money got made through real estate. But that isn't all we did.

Technically, very little of our business is legal. But that's just the particulars.

Laws change all the time. What's illegal today might be legal tomorrow. Seriously, it's lawmakers who are some of the shadiest fuckers around.

Especially on the East Coast. Politicians are just so slimy. I hated doing business with them.

But they're a necessary evil. Like me.

I keep my territory the way I like it. Sure, everyone has vices, and we run some of them.

Gambling, drugs, sex.

That's small change stuff. But that is what brings Sam Keller to my door.

He likes to gamble. On anything from horses to sports to fights. He's got bad luck though, and it makes me itch.

The first time I see him, I want to rub the malocchio tattoo on my right arm, but I don't. I keep still. I show no emotion.

I can't.

"This one's trouble, Boss," Angel says, and I nod. He is.

But I let him in. I took his marker.

Weeks passed since Sam Keller made his first bet. And now, I fucking own him.

We're not the only game in town, but we're the ones with the worst rep. I don't know why he picked us.

This close to New York City, there's always something brewing. I let other guys have their say on that side of the Hudson, but here I'm the king.

Anyone who's anyone knows it and they don't cross me.

Not unless they want to end up dead. Not boasting, just stating facts.

I'm not an arrogant fuck. I know there are other organizations led by other men.

But we operate in complete symbiosis. We have to. There is no other option.

Our rep keeps us safe and the fact that I'll do any fucking thing I have to in order to keep whatever I deem mine safe.

You fuck with a Viper, you get bit. That's something no one survives.

Period.

I earned my crown through blood, sweat, and cunning. I live in a world shrouded in darkness, built on shady promises and lies.

In that kind of world, you learn not to trust. Not to want things you can't have.

But I'm the king. I can have anything I want, I just need the balls to take it.

And what I want is Sam Keller's sister.

I might not have a Harvard degree, but I wasn't born yesterday. I don't take unnecessary risks.

The day he made his first wager, I had Sam Keller checked out. I know he is technically part owner in the old school bread bakery his sister is practically killing herself to keep afloat.

Anna Keller is a fucking angel. She's beautiful. Soft, sweet, but she has a backbone, too.

You have to in order to run a business like that. Especially when she has no help.

Sam doesn't carry his weight, and Anna works too hard.

He's a little douchebag is what he is.

A selfish leech.

A fucking tick.

But she, well, Anna Keller is something else. She's tough.

Beautiful.

A flower among the thorns of the hard city we live in. Something about her draws me in and I'm curious.

I'm not the kind of man who walks up to a woman and just asks her out. That's just not me.

I can't let anyone in. I have to be strong for my men. I have to be ruthless in order to keep my crown.

Anna is soft.

Precious.

I shouldn't be thinking about her, but I can't stop. She works too hard, and I'm not about to make her life harder by pretending I could somehow fit into it.

I can't.

I won't even try.

But I'm not a good man, either.

I'm a viper.

So, in my den I wait for the opportunity to strike, to take what I want.

I'm the puppet-master pulling all the strings. I let Sam have just enough rope to get himself caught, but I won't hang him. Not as long as he plays ball.

And he does. The asshole gives up his sister with hardly a protest when I call in his debt.

It makes me furious. He doesn't deserve a sister like that.

It also makes me hard.

For her.

Tonight is the night. She's here.

That sweet little thing is walking right into my trap.

I should feel guilty, but I don't.

My dick gets hard as I watch her on the security monitor enter my office in the basement of the Vipers' Den.

Office is a loose term. Yeah, there's a desk. But there's also a bedroom.

Not because it's my fuck room, but because sometimes I need to crash and going home to my empty condo gets more and more difficult.

I hate being needy. This woman makes me needy.

She makes me wonder what it would be like to have someone soft and precious waiting for me in that big condo.

I watch her through the monitor as she slowly progresses, getting closer to me with every step, and I'm not even breathing regularly anymore.

Her big brown eyes flick up to the ceiling, and I swear she knows I'm watching. It's like she can see the camera, even though I know she can't.

It's been expertly hidden in the rafters. Not even trained professionals manage to spot this one.

Goddamn. Her eyes are so beautiful.

She's so close I can see their whisky brown color and the flecks of gold glittering inside them, making her look like something from a dream or fantasy.

I hear Angel give her my orders. Telling her to strip, and my dick is jumping behind my jeans.

Jaw clenched, I watch as the beauty walks into the bedroom.

Her shoulders lift as she takes a deep inhale and I switch to the camera inside the bedroom.

It's a private feed. I'm the only one with the code.

Good thing too, because the moment she takes off her coat and starts to remove her clothes, I'm drowning in a dozen different emotions.

The least of which is not jealousy.

I know she's thirty-two. Her parents are both gone, and she's been trying her best to raise her piece-of-shit brother and keep the bakery from falling down around their heads.

She works a lot. She doesn't date.

Probably has some fucked up idea in her head that she isn't gorgeous because she's so thick.

But she is.

And it pisses me off to even imagine she might not agree.

Anna looks exactly how a woman should. I'm glad she's single, but it wouldn't matter.

I take what I want.

She's taking off her shirt, and her hands go to her pants. She has a pair of tights, and when she pulls them off, she takes her panties with them.

Soft, pale skin is revealed, inch by inch, and I wish I was the one unwrapping her.

When she stands up again, I take her in. I can't wait to touch her.

To taste her.

I want to run my tongue across every inch, every dip and curve of her body.

Fuck.

Blood rushes to my cock, and I hear it roaring as it races through my veins.

Anna is perfect.

And for tonight, she's mine.

CHAPTER FOUR-ANNA

One entire wall is lined in mirrors and it's nerve wracking.

Is this guy some kind of pervert?

I roll my eyes. I mean, obviously.

I hear a lock clicking and a doorknob turning, and it's loud like a firecracker.

I startle and move to cover myself with my hands.

"Drop your hands," a deep, gravelly voice commands one second before I see him.

Holy. Shit.

My breath freezes in my lungs as I take in the enormous figure of a man standing in the doorway. He's still cloaked in shadows, but one more step inside the bedroom, and I can really see him.

He's huge. At least a foot taller than me, and thick ropes of muscle cover his arms and torso.

He's only wearing jeans, and damn, they look like they are struggling to contain him. But his face. It's familiar.

"You look like Angel," I blurt.

He dips his chin, and it looks like he's going to smile. But he doesn't.

"Angel is my cousin and my second. My name is Nico," he replies. "Do you know why you're here, Anna Keller? Do you understand what you're here to do?"

I lick my lips, my mouth suddenly dry. His voice is so rich and masculine, I swear he should narrate audiobooks or something. I press my legs together, hopefully in a way that doesn't draw attention.

But his gaze drops to my thighs, or maybe he's looking at the close-cropped curls covering my sex, so I guess I failed to be inconspicuous.

"I'm, um, here to pay a debt. To give you my body for one night in return for wiping my brother's bill clean."

He nods. His eyes never leave mine.

He steps forward, raising his big, inked up hands to my face. His nostrils flare and my eyes go wide when I feel him wrap his long fingers around my throat.

"Why are you doing this for him, huh? Your brother is a piece of shit," he growls, startling me.

"He's my brother."

It's the only answer I have. But I can see it makes him angry. Or maybe that's disgust marring his otherwise handsome features.

He steps back, releasing me, and I can breathe more easily. But I'm cold without his hands on me. And I'm very aware that's not something I should be feeling.

His gaze rakes over me from head to toe, not lingering anywhere in particular. I'm a little disappointed but not surprised.

The man, *Nico*, looks like he's chiseled from marble. I feel flabby and unworthy by comparison.

I'm nothing special.

And yet, there I am. Butt ass naked. Standing in front of a crime lord built like a superhero.

I'm nervous. I might start sweating, and God knows, my knees are knocking.

I can't help but wonder what I'm supposed to do next.

Good thing I don't have to wonder for long.

"Get on the bed. On your hands and knees. Face the wall."

His words are clipped, and I know I'm right. He is angry.

But I do as he says, a sliver of nervous anticipation works its way through my body, stopping somewhere in my core.

It's been a long time for me, and he's a really good-looking guy. The kind of man I fantasize about when I'm reading romance novels and picturing myself as the heroine.

Yeah, his body is amazing. He's just so ripped. But he has scars, too. And I know those muscles aren't just for show.

He's handsome, too. His nose is straight. His chin defined. He has high cheekbones and perfect lips. But it's his eyes that really caught my attention.

They're bright blue and stunning.

Still. Nothing about him or this sick little exchange should turn me on.

I'm basically prostituting myself. Giving my body to him in exchange for clearing Sammy's debt.

Shit. I'm so mad at him. So disappointed in my brother.

And I want to hate this guy for letting Sammy do

it. For taking his marker when he clearly doesn't have the experience to make such bets.

But I can't blame Nico. He is what he is.

King of the Vipers.

"I said, get on the bed, Rosebud," he growls.

My stomach clenches and I move to obey his commands, trying not to care that my soft body is completely bare to him.

I'm shocked, and a little embarrassed. I know this position will expose my sex to this stranger, and he'll see it.

He'll know I'm *excited.*

I close my eyes and inhale a shaky breath as I lean forward until I'm positioned on my hands and knees, facing the exposed brick wall.

I hear the rustling of his jeans as he shucks them off. I suck in another breath as the bed depresses when he joins me on top of the mattress.

The comforter is slate gray, thick, expensive. It feels nice beneath my hands.

"Relax, Anna. I won't hurt you."

Then I feel his hands on my body. He's touching my back, tracing lines down my spine, conjuring shivers, and making me ache.

"You're so fucking soft. I knew you would be," he murmurs.

My eyes close as he does it again. Nico runs his big hands down my sides this time, over my hips, tracing the globes of my ass, all the way down to my knees.

Then his fingers trace along my inner thighs, and suddenly, he's pressing my legs apart.

"Fuck," he grunts. "You're fucking soaked, Rosebud."

I don't understand the nickname or why he's given it to me. But I can't find the air necessary to speak because Nico is kneeling behind me.

"Look at you all pink and wet for me. Gotta see if you taste as good as you look."

His big hands are holding my thighs apart, my pussy on display, and fuck, I think I feel his warm breath on my skin before I feel him press his mouth against me.

A keening moan escapes my lips and I clutch the blankets beneath my hands.

I expect him to come at me like a beast. But I don't expect this. Hell, I don't even know what *this* is.

I'm not a virgin, no, but this is beyond my experience.

Nico is everywhere. His mouth, his tongue, his hands. He moans as he eats me out from pussy to asshole and I don't know what to do with any of it.

So, I just hold on and let the big, bad Viper have his way with me.

The fact that I love what he's doing is something I'll never tell. I can't. It's just not something I can reconcile in my brain.

Nico is a criminal. He's not the kind of guy I date, if I was dating anyone.

My brain is scrambling to catch up to the way he's making my body feel.

I should have mercy on myself.

I should lie and tell myself I'm letting him ravage me all for Sammy's sake.

That's probably for the best. But I never was a good liar. And when he asks me if it feels good, I answer.

And I beg for more.

"Y-yes. It feels so good, Nico. Please."

CHAPTER FIVE-NICO

Let's get one thing clear, I tell my conscience as it starts to rear its ugly head, *I have every intention of fucking Anna Keller tonight*

Obsessions aren't a good thing for a man like me to have. I have to admit, since I learned of her existence, I've been more than a little preoccupied with the curvy beauty.

I'm not a good man. Pushing forty, I'm the king of one of the most hated criminal organizations on the Eastern Seaboard. The Vipers have fingers in a lot of pies.

But we grease the right palms, we keep business smooth and only take out the trash that fucking deserves it. So, the authorities are happy to look the other way.

Stalking someone isn't exactly my thing. But I've been creeping into Anna Keller's life without her knowing ever since little Sammy started playing in the Den.

Yeah, I knew he was getting in over his head. But I allowed her brother to run up a tab with one sole purpose.

And that's getting Anna into my bed without all the hassle of wooing and pretending to be something I'm not.

I can't offer her anything.

Nothing more than a ride on my dick. And something tells me that's not Anna's style. I still want her, though.

And even though I'm pissed she's willing to give in to me for her shithead brother's sake, I'm gonna take her.

If she wants to be a sacrifice, who am I to refuse?

I'm not a good enough man to say no. Especially not when her pink pussy is glistening, fucking soaked, and all for me.

Jesus Christ.

I want to make a meal out of her. I can't help myself. I gotta taste her.

But I'm not satisfied with her juices coating my

tongue and lips. No, I need to hear how much this good little girl likes it when I tongue fuck her.

I have to hear her tell me how it feels when I lick into her sweet, dripping cunt. Need to know if she wants me to eat her ass, which I'm gonna do, anyway. So, right before I lick her asshole, I ask her.

"Taste so good. Does it feel good? Gonna eat this ass next, Mama. You want that? Tell me."

"Y-yes. God, yes. It feels so good, Nico. Please."

Anna is on her knees, and she is begging me.

Fucking begging me.

I groan, and I bite her cheek, her moan echoing around the room as my tongue slides between her slick folds.

She tastes so fucking good.

Like promises. Like hunger.

Desire.

And relief once my mouth is on her.

I can't take it anymore. I move, lining my cock with her slick entrance. Lust consumes me.

It's been a while for me. I haven't touched a woman since I saw a picture of her.

My Anna.

No. Not mine.

It's important I keep that in mind. She isn't mine

to keep. There's no place for roses in my world. Except maybe at funerals.

And that's a thought I refuse to acknowledge.

Anna is sweet, good, and pure. She's way too good for me.

But I don't fucking care. Not tonight.

Tonight, I need to feel her pussy convulsing around me.

"Fuck, Rosebud, you're so tight. Goddamn."

I slam my hips against her soft ass. For a second, I wished I had her on her back so I could see the expression that went with her yell.

She's stiff at first. Like she can't possibly comprehend her body's reaction to mine.

But I know women, and I can feel how desperate she is to have me.

My poor pretty Rosebud.

It's been a long time for her, too. I hate the thought of other men touching her, but I'm glad it's me tonight. Glad I'm the one who's knocking her socks off.

I reach around and find her clit with my fingers, strumming the tiny little nub until she's squirming and pushing back into my thrusts.

"That's it. Give it to me," I grunt, taking her harder with each pass.

Her body is warm and soft and jiggling against me, and it's the best damn thing I ever felt. I turn my head, watching her in the mirror, and the sight is so damn sexy, I almost come.

But I need her there with me. I pull out, grabbing her wide hips, I flip Anna over onto her back. Her big whiskey eyes are lust-glazed and she's panting.

So fucking pretty.

I press her legs wide apart, and I slam back inside her, catching her cries with my mouth.

It's the first time I kiss her, and she gifts me with a flood of warmth where my dick is stroking deep inside her.

So this is what she needs. My little Rosebud craves kisses.

Well, I can do that.

I cup her face, angling her head, I deepen the kiss, not letting her up for air for even a second.

I just keep licking into her, savoring her flavors, memorizing each one. I suck on her lips, making plucking sounds as I release one only to claim the other. Then I nibble my way down her chin, and neck, to her big tits, sucking one nipple into my mouth.

I want to devour her. I want to consume every single inch. Stamp myself all over.

But I can't keep her. And the knowledge is making me fucking furious.

"Fuck, Rosebud, this pussy was made for me. Tell me," I grunt, licking a trail from her neck all the way up her cheek.

"Nico," she says my name and fuck, I'm not ready for how much it affects me.

My cock pulses, and I rear up onto my knees.

"That's it. Squeeze my cock with your cunt, but I want you to strum that clit when you do it. Now, Anna."

Her breathing is labored, but I watch in awe as she obeys.

Three swipes across her needy little bud, and Anna is coming all over me. Which is a good thing, cause I'm right there with her.

I come so hard, I damn near pass out. It's all I can do not to crush her beneath my weight as I collapse on top of her soft, warm body.

Usually I need some recovery time between bouts, but my dick is already hard again. And Anna's soft moan tells me she feels it, too.

"Slow this time, I think," I say to no one in particular.

I kiss Anna. My eyes open and on hers as I start to move my hips, rocking into her.

The mess of our combined release coats my way, making it easier to slide in and out, and fuck it feels good.

I know she's on birth control. I hacked into her medical records, so I also know her last checkup was two weeks ago, and her blood work came back normal.

Just like I know I'm clean, too.

I never fuck a woman without a condom, but there's something about her that won't allow me to do it any other way but raw.

I need all of her. Need to feel all of her.

We come together this time. My cock pulses inside her just as her pussy tightens, her walls sucking the cum right from my balls.

It feels—it feels good. Really good.

Being inside her is better than anything else I have ever felt. Anna trembles and I hold her to me.

We're practically strangers. Everything I know about her, I stole. But she doesn't feel like a stranger.

She feels big.

Important.

"I got you," I whisper, wrapping my arms around her as she continues to quiver around me.

Matters of the heart are alien to me, but business

deals I could handle. That's all this is, I remind myself.

But I also remind myself I'm a fucking liar.

My body is ready for her again and isn't that fucking new? I thought maybe sex had simply lost its spark for me.

But not with her. She is different. And it feels like maybe I could be different with her. Or pretend to be, at the very least.

Just for tonight.

This woman is throwing my wavering libido a lifeline, and I am a selfish prick through and through, so I'll take it.

I'll take everything she offers.

I press my nose to her hair and breathe her scent. She smells fresh and clean, like maybe she showered before she came here.

Her shampoo is floral, but not overbearing, and I like it. I breathe her in again, this time with my mouth open, savoring her essence on my tongue.

I thought one night of fucking would be enough to work out my need for this woman.

But I'm thinking I'm wrong.

So, instead of kicking her out like planned, I wrap her in my arms and tuck her close to my body, fighting to stay awake.

I found a sense of peace in Anna's warmth I never expected. And I'm not ready to say goodbye just yet.

Lulled into the first deep sleep I had in years, I wake up hours later. Alone.

"Fuck," I growl and heft myself out of bed, going right for the security feed on my laptop.

I don't bother with clothes. No one is in my office. Not without my permission. No one would dare.

I watch the feed showing Anna as she dressed and left just a few hours ago. She paused by my bed, kissing my head before she takes off and I press my hand over my heart.

That long dead thing starts to pound.

She kissed me. Why?

"I wasn't ready for you to leave," I say to myself.

Unfortunately, she took the decision out of my hands when she disappeared.

Business matters take my attention for the rest of the day, but I can't stop thinking about my little Rosebud.

One night didn't quench my desire for her. But she's gone. And I'm not sure if I should hunt her down. Honestly, it would be a mercy to let her go.

But I don't know if I have it in me to be merciful anymore.

CHAPTER SIX-ANNA

Six months later

I enter my apartment with a sigh as I walk to turn on the AC. It's a cheap window unit, and I don't even know if it still works.

But I hope it does. New Jersey summers are a mixed bag, but it looks like I came back to a freaking heat wave.

I miss Pancake, but I know the family who adopted him from me are good people. They're treating him well, and they even send me updates every now and then.

It makes me sad, but I know it's for the best. My allergies have been a little loopy just lately.

So has everything else.

I spent the last six months hiding out in the

condo my best friend's family owns in Florida. Giselle is still pissed at me. I never explained why I ran away, but I knew she'd help.

We go way back. More like sisters than friends. Always there for each other. That's been our promise since we started first grade over at St. Lucy's Parochial School.

So when I asked, she handed me the keys immediately. There's no one like Giselle.

Damn.

I realize how much I missed her over the past several months.

My heart squeezes inside my chest, and I suck in a sharp breath. I don't know if I can do this alone.

But I don't really have a choice.

Giselle has already done too much for me, allowing me the use of her family's vacation home without question. She is a busy person with a thriving career in social media marketing.

I can't even pretend to know what that is. She's tried to set up accounts for me for the bakery, but I can't pay her, so I won't allow it.

I won't abuse our friendship that way. Even if I do give her parents bread whenever they're in town.

It's just not the same.

Her parents only use the condo during the summer. So, it was a good run while it lasted.

June just rolled around, and I booked my ticket and came back. Giselle's parents arrived shortly after I left.

I already got their text thanking me for the fresh rolls I baked and left on the counter, and for cleaning the place.

Anyway, I just can't stay away any longer. Can't run forever.

Sammy's latest round of voicemails made no sense at all, and I know I need to see my brother to figure out what the heck he's doing and to tell him I'm done.

The air inside my apartment is stale. The AC is blowing cold, so I thank God for that.

Thoughts of my brother gnaw at my mind, but it's no good. No matter how I feel about him I need to draw the line.

Sammy is an adult. He makes his own choices with no thought for me or anyone else.

My heart hurts when I think this, but it's the only option left. I just can't worry about him anymore. I can't put my life aside for him.

Not anymore.

Because it's not just me I need to consider. I have someone else to watch out for now.

My hand goes to the bump beneath my breasts, and I can't help but smile when I feel the flutter of life growing within my belly.

The thing about being a big girl is I'm only starting to look pregnant now as I enter my third trimester.

Before, I simply looked fat. Maybe it's because of all the morning sickness. I didn't expect to have that cute little basketball belly skinny women have when they are pregnant, but still.

I am thrilled now that I can see what the doctors and the half dozen home tests I took told me.

I am pregnant. With Nico Fury's baby.

Like every other time I think about him, my pulse races and my heart thuds heavily against my ribs.

When I took off on New Year's Day, I expected to return after a few weeks. I thought I was just going down to Fort Lauderdale to get my head on straight.

But once I started losing my breakfast, my plans pivoted.

Noise in the hall brings my head up and I brace myself.

"Anna? You better be ready to explain what the hell is going on—"

Giselle pushes my front door open, and I can see from her expression my bestie is still pissed at me.

Then her gaze drops to my belly, and she gasps.

"Hi," I whisper, my eyes filling with tears.

"Oh my God! Anna, you're pregnant!"

"Yeah, I know." I sniff and roll my eyes.

"Holy fuck! Okay, first," she says, grabbing my hands, "are you okay?"

"Yeah. I'm good. Sammy?"

I ask, hoping she's been able to track him down for me. He hasn't answered my last few texts, and I'm worried.

Giselle's face falls, and I know she's keeping something from me. But I can be patient when I have to be. And I know my bestie won't be rushed.

So, I sit, and I rub my palms over my belly.

I allow myself a moment to enjoy the cool air coming from the air conditioner. And I wait.

Giselle places a thick black binder held together with rubber bands on the table. She frowns. Then she tucks her dark locks behind her ears.

I don't know how she has all that hair down in this heat. It's only the first week of June, and I actually cringe when I think about what it's going to be like over the next few weeks.

Being pregnant and alone in the hot humid city is going to be hell on me. I just know it.

Sadness fills me as my thoughts strayed back to Sammy. I just can't take the stress of his problems added to mine.

I have no more savings, and the bakers are trying to push me out of the business entirely.

Not to mention, there's this whole thing where I have to avoid my baby's father.

How the hell am I gonna do that?

The research I've done on Nico Fury and the Vipers has garnered little information. I know he's suspected of being the head of a crime syndicate.

But what the heck does that even mean?

Was he like the Godfather or something?

He sure as heck didn't resemble an old timey mafioso. Not with all those tattoos and muscles.

Stop it.

I remind myself I'm not alone, and now is not the time to go fantasizing about what was probably the best sex I have ever had.

Another thing I didn't know about pregnancy was how the hormone surges increased a woman's sex drive at the most inopportune times.

Go figure.

"Before we get into that, I want you to know I have the books from Theresa. She really did a good job filling your shoes as manager for the bakery. But you were right, Anna. They want you out. Javi and the bakers don't want to pay you a cut anymore. They just want you gone."

"Fuck," I moan, closing my eyes.

Talk about problems. The tiny bit of money I make with my family's bakery is a pittance.

But the bakery is my legacy.

Mine and Sammy's.

Not that he ever cared.

"But we can talk about them later. First, tell me everything about you getting knocked up. And don't you dare fucking lie," she demands.

"Fine, But you're not gonna like it, Sisi," I murmur, calling her by her nickname.

I start at the beginning, with Sammy owing money to the Vipers.

And I end my story with me inside the king of the Vipers' bed, where he makes me come more times than I could count, and subsequently gets me pregnant.

"Are you fucking serious?" she asks, thirty minutes later when I finally finish telling my tale.

"Um, yeah, Sisi, I'm pretty fucking serious."

I gesture to my stomach.

"Well, from your description of him, at least the baby should be cute," she says, lifting one shoulder. "Unless all that ink his daddy has makes him come out with like blue skin or some shit."

"Oh my God, what is wrong with you?"

I laugh. Then I cry.

I blame it on hormones, but it's more than that.

"Hey, it'll be okay. Aunt Sisi is gonna take care of you both," she says and before I know it, my bestie is hugging me.

I cling to her, so grateful for human contact. Six months without even a single physical touch was rough on me.

I like hugs. Not that I'd been hugged very often, but I know I like them.

I crave human contact.

I can't wait for my baby to arrive. To have the chance to cuddle them and give them all the love I know I'm capable of.

I huff a breath and shake my head, wiping the stray tears that are rolling down my face.

"So, what's the plan?"

"The plan?" I look at her, utterly confused.

"Yeah, are you gonna tell him?"

"Him who? Nico? No! Why would I?"

Hope. Horror. Angst. Need. Fear.

One by one, emotions flitter through me and I'm practically gasping by the time Giselle responds.

"Um, because he's the father. He has rights, and so do you. The bakers aren't gonna pay you much longer. They're threatening to quit unless you agree to sign over ownership of the business to them. This Nico is the dad, right? So, he has to pay child support," she says, like I'm dumb.

"The bakers are my problem. If they want me gone, I will sell the business to them and the bread routes, but they aren't pushing me out for nothing. Besides, I don't own this building. There are three mortgages on it. If they think I'm just going to give it to them, they're crazy."

"And what about Daddy dearest?" Giselle pushes, and my stomach turns.

"What about him, Sisi? This isn't his business—"

Something shatters in the other room, and I am on my feet. Giselle grabs me by the hand, stopping me from going inside.

"Wait." she hisses, and she is already dialing 911.

I hear a groan and a couple of loud thuds. Someone laughs, and the sound is pure evil.

I shake Giselle's hand off me. Somewhere in the back of my mind I recognize that groan.

Fear trickles up my spine as I walk through my bedroom.

The window in my tiny bedroom is shattered, but I walk towards it and look outside.

I peer through the darkness to where shadows are moving almost out of my line of vision.

I see something. It's crawling through the trash bags sitting on the sidewalk, waiting for pickup tomorrow morning.

Something scurries between the heavy black plastic. Probably a rat.

My attention flicks back to the huddled mass. It pauses and I think I recognize the brown shirt with the cream letters on the back. I can't read what it says.

There's something dark and thick, and it's leaking all over the mass and it takes me a moment to discern it's a person.

The liquid pooling beneath them is like chocolate syrup. They finally stop moving just beneath the flickering streetlight.

Then, I scream.

CHAPTER SEVEN-NICO

"What do we fucking know about this?" I bark.

"Warehouse is gone. Staz, the night guard, saw them creeping around with Molotov cocktails and called it in after he got to safety," Luc answers first.

"And?"

"And Sanchez fucking junior doesn't care what was mapped out with his father. He's claiming this is his turf," Angel explains.

Pure rage leaks into my vision. This fucking punk.

I look at the footage of what's left of one of my warehouses and I fume. This prick set fire to it.

He's lucky no one was injured. Lucky it was empty. But that's not the fucking point.

"Want us to hit him back?" Angel asks.

My gaze flicks to Luc who's still studying the footage. He is frowning, and I wait for him to speak.

Angel is my muscle guy. My cousin. My best friend. And Luc. Luc is my Council. Looking at him, you wouldn't think he graduated from Princeton Law.

He's wiry and tall, but his lean build belies his strength. I've known Luc a long time. Since we were both kids causing trouble for the dealers on our block growing up.

His sister OD'd before her twenty-first birthday, which was a year after my mother had done the same. Back then we didn't know what we were doing. We were just angry.

The cops wouldn't help, so we did it ourselves. We raided stash house. Chased away customers. Started fucking fights.

My cousin, Angel, joined us after I got my ass handed to me. Then he started training us. We learned to box. To shoot. To fight with knives.

Little by little, with Luc and Angel by my side, I built an underworld army. And with that army, I cut out a chunk of territory for us, for the Vipers.

The Den is just our base of operations.

Anyone wanting to play on our turf had to pay the piper, but there was some shit I just didn't allow.

Like this fucking fentanyl bullshit. An opioid epidemic, that's what they called it.

Some blamed the dealers. Some blamed the politicians.

But I don't give a fuck whose fault it was.

People want to escape. They have for years, and whether it's drinking, drugs, gambling, sex, or violence, they're gonna have their outlets.

People with vices weren't going away.

But the means by which people escaped can be controlled. They can be regulated.

Someone with enough balls could take charge of the pushers and the truly evil leeches that fed off human misery.

I'm not a fucking judge. And I'm not God, either. What I am is the motherfucking king of the Vipers.

I make the rules.

And if that little pissant Sanchez Junior thinks he can destroy my property and get away with it. He's wrong.

So fucking wrong.

I give my orders to Angel, and he nods, showing me he understands. He's my Enforcer. The head muscle guy and I have no doubt he'll do what I say.

He's too good at it not to. Angel leaves my office, and I feel a sense of excitement bubbling in my veins.

I always feel like that when something is about to happen. So, this makes sense.

Sanchez wants a fucking war, but he's not going to get one.

The Vipers don't just strike back.

We destroy.

We decimate.

We are the scourge that leaves nothing behind.

I exhale and roll my neck. Control is hard earned, but I mastered that technique long ago.

Luc is quiet, but that's nothing new. His eyes are trained on the security monitors while I cipher through my thoughts.

My eyes flick to the bedroom door in my office and I steel myself against the unwanted emotions coiling through me.

Six months ago I had her in my bed, and then she vanished without a trace.

Anna Keller is the very definition of the one that got away.

But maybe it's for the better.

Every time I think about tracking her down. Something stops me.

I might think it's my conscience if I had one of those. But there's no voice in my head telling me what's right and wrong.

No Jiminy Cricket motherfucker telling me what to do. To leave her alone.

Still, what could I give her?

Before I can fall down the rabbit hole of the ifs and buts of pursuing Anna Keller, I hear Luc snort.

"What?"

"You know that little flower who came in here six months ago to pay off her brother's debts?"

"Yeah," I reply, and I lean forward.

"Well, I think she just walked in, and uh, Boss, she's got a surprise."

My heart is hammering. She's back. Anna is back in town, and she is here. In my place.

I don't care what brought her here. I just know I want her. Six months did nothing to dampen my need for this woman.

"Boss?"

"I got it," I say.

Then I stand.

CHAPTER EIGHT-ANNA

F ear slithers down my soul as I stare at the enormous sign featuring a coiled up black snake ready to strike.

I've seen it once before, but last time was a walk in the park compared to how I feel now.

I walk into the Vipers' Den and my gaze flits around from one hulking man to the next. I don't know if *he's* here.

And really, I am not so sure I should be, either. My hands go to my belly, and I feel a protective wave roll over me, forcing me to reject any uncertainty.

I'm not here for me. Besides, I have nowhere else to turn and the police already said they couldn't do anything without witnesses.

I'm exhausted and my throat is sore from crying and talking to the police.

After I recognized the huddled form below my window as belonging to my brother, I ran down the stairs from my apartment to see if I could help him. And to wait for the cops and ambulance to arrive.

Sammy.

Images of my brother and the sweet baby he used to be filter through my brain. My heart hurts so badly, I sway on my feet.

Oh, Sammy. Why?

"What are you doing here? Oh my God, are you pregnant?" a sharp female voice snaps.

I turn my head to see the pretty bartender I remember from the first and only other time I ever went to the Vipers' Den glaring at me. Her eyes are glued to my stomach, and her expression is sour.

"I, uh, can you tell Nico—"

"You think you're the first woman to trick the king with fake paternity suits? You better get your ass outta here," she says, but her warning is flat.

"I-I need to see him," I reply, finding my backbone somewhere beneath the numbness disguising my pain.

"Anna."

I turn my head and see Nico striding towards me.

He looks like some reigning monarch, his black on black outfit is molded to his perfect body.

His short-sleeved shirt is tight, showing off his incredible biceps and pecs, hinting at the abs beneath the fabric.

His fitted pants are just as fantastic, showing just how powerful and thick his legs are.

I've seen him naked. I know what he looks like, and I appreciate him for all his masculine beauty.

But it's not Nico's good looks that leave me speechless. It's the hardness I see in his eyes.

He looks upset.

Angry.

Oh wow. He looks so fucking mad. But I don't know if it's at me or what?

Why should he be angry with me?

I am nothing to him. I'm just someone he once fucked. No biggie, right?

To guys like him, I'm a dime a dozen. Another notch on his bedpost. But why do I have the feeling he is mad at me?

Scantily clad women pose and gasp, each of them vying for his attention. I feel sick to my stomach, wondering how many he's slept with since I skipped town.

It's not fair of me. I have no right. But I can't help it.

But for all their beauty and all their silicone-enhanced assets blatantly on display, I can see for myself that Nico is not looking at them.

He's looking at me.

And suddenly, I feel warm. Like really warm.

His eyes are burning like blue flames as he closes the distance between us.

I gape, mouth open. I can't help it. Tattoos dance across his skin like shadows in the dim light and I can barely make them out, but I know what they are.

He stops right in front of me, completely invading my personal space.

I haven't seen or spoken to Nico since New Year's Eve.

But my body lights up, like it recognizes its master. I feel his warm breath on my forehead as he bends his head and puts his hand on my belly.

My eyes widen. My waist is thick. The child we created is stretching my already soft flesh.

The baby kicks. And I know he can feel it.

"My office. Now," he says, his voice so damn deep.

He drops his hand, like it burns, and walks away,

leaving me to trail behind him. It's like he doesn't even worry I won't obey him.

That's when I notice all the other eyes on me, and I realize he's right.

With all his men watching me, creating a barrier between me and the rest of the bar goers, I follow him. I have no other choice.

He's talking into a cell phone, and I swear I hear him say "Get me Preacher".

But I'm not sure.

When we get inside his office, he takes my purse and I think he's gonna hang it up, but instead, he goes through my wallet and takes out my driver's license.

"What are you doing?"

He ignores me. His phone rings as he answers it.

"Bring him down."

"Nico?" I interrupt, not understanding what is happening.

He hasn't even given me a chance to explain.

"I only want to hear two words from you. I and do," he growls, and I gasp.

"What? You're crazy." I shake my head.

"You have no fucking idea. But I guarantee you no kid of mine is coming into this world a bastard."

What the heck is going on? Is he serious?

"Nico, that's not why I'm here. You can't just—"

"You telling me that baby isn't mine?" he asks, and he is so mad.

I tremble. But I'm not afraid. In fact, I think I'm turned on. Inside his office, I can hardly hear the music from the bar.

But I feel something in the air between us. An electrical charge. An energy. A vibrance I have never felt with anyone else.

I'm just as sick as him.

"No," I say honestly, because I can't lie to him.

I just can't.

"I'm not saying that, but I'm here cause, well, Sammy's dead."

"What? How?"

"Someone dumped him outside my apartment earlier tonight. He was beaten, stabbed, and h-he didn't make it," I say, grief hitting me all over again.

"Fuck."

I feel Nico's hands on my shoulders as he guides me to a chair.

"When did you get back to town?"

"This afternoon. How did you know I was gone?"

He doesn't answer.

"Do you know the name of the cop working the

case? Or what hospital he was taken to? Never mind. I'll find out."

"I-I, I mean, they threw this through my window."

I take the rock out of my pocket and hand it to him. I don't know why I didn't give it to the cops, but here I am now, so my reasons don't matter.

Nico takes it from me. At first, it looks like an ordinary rock. About four inches long and half as wide. Nothing special.

But then he turns it over and sees it. Drawn right on top is the unmistakable image of a snake with a knife stabbing it through the head.

A dangerous energy sizzles in the air. It's raw and unbridled, purely masculine in its tone and demeanor.

It takes me a moment to realize it's him. That feeling of heaviness is simply Nico.

I wonder if Fury is his real name or if he chose it. Either way, it's apt because he is the very definition of fury in that moment.

His anger is so damn strong, it's palpable.

"I don't know what that means, but it feels bad. I-I came to you for protection."

I finally find my voice as Nico's blue eyes flash to mine. He cocks his head to the side, like a wild animal, and my heart hammers harder against my ribs.

Someone knocks on the door, and he growls a command for them to enter. An older man with a familiar collar comes in, followed by one of the men I saw upstairs.

A priest?

"What do you need to marry us?" Nico addresses the priest.

"What?" The priest looks shocked.

"Do I need to repeat myself?"

"No, no. Um, you just need to file a license and have someone perform the ceremony with witnesses. I have a license in here," he says and takes a paper out of the case he's holding.

"Good. Give it," Nico grunts and takes the paper.

I sit stunned while he fills it in. Nico uses a complicated looking multifunction machine to make copies of his and my driver's licenses, along with the actual wedding application.

I should argue. Or something. But I'm actually just stunned.

"Okay, here. Now do it," he says.

"W-why are you doing this? I'm here because I have to find my brother's killer and to protect my baby against them."

"Your brother don't need you looking out for him anymore, Rosebud."

I gasp. It hurts to hear him say it so frankly, but he's right.

Sammy made his choices, and he's paid for them. With his life.

"Look, I'm sorry if that came out rough, but it's the truth. And you clearly need someone looking out for you. Walking in this fucking place alone and pregnant," Nico growls.

I feel the flash of anger rise in him even as he tries to stanch its growth. Then he's standing in front of me.

His body is so close I can feel the power vibrating off him. He crouches, taking my trembling hands in his.

"You came to me for protection. This is how we do it. You take my name, Anna Keller, you keep growing my baby in your belly, but you do it under my roof. Where I can keep you both safe. But first, you're gonna marry me. Okay?"

"Okay," I say, nodding my head as tears spill down my cheeks.

"Good. You look thin. Luc, I want you to get me the best OBGYN on staff at the Medical Center," he says to his man, naming a local hospital.

"Yes, boss."

"I, uh, I have a doctor—"

"Nonnegotiable. From now on your body is a goddamn temple. Only the best, Anna. I won't tolerate less."

"How, uh, how do you know the baby is yours?"

He just looks at me as if to say, "who else got you pregnant". I huff. I'm being petulant, but whatever.

Truth is, I can't help but feel relieved. It's crazy. I know it is. That I am even considering marrying this guy is likely the result of some borderline personality disorder, I'm sure of it.

But I've been so alone lately. And it feels kind of nice to have someone to share it with. All the joys and worries of pregnancy.

With this new threat, well, I'm actually glad Nico is here and stepping up.

Who knew mafia types could be so Gung-ho to marry one night stands that end up in surprise pregnancies?

The preacher finishes looking over the papers, and he gestures the other man forward.

"Luc, are you witnessing?"

"Yes," the man, Luc, answers.

He bends down and signs the papers. Then hands the pen to Nico. Nico signs and hands the pen and paper to me.

I sit there staring at the document.

"Sign it, Rosebud."

He's back to crouching in front of me as he gives the order and the dark timber of his voice sends shivers down my spine.

I grip the pen. Nico presses down on my hand gently, forcing the felt tip to the paper.

I take a breath.

And I sign.

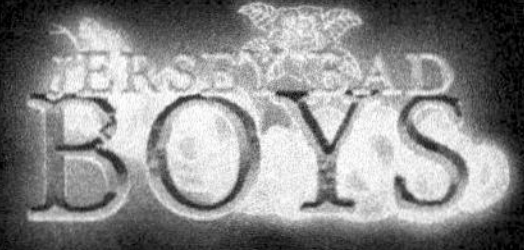

CHAPTER NINE-NICO

My entire body is vibrating as I watch Anna sign her name to the marriage license.

It's brash and reckless. Stupid? Maybe. But I don't give a fuck what anyone thinks.

That's my baby she's carrying beneath her breast, and I want it. I won't acknowledge the part where I want Anna just as much.

I haven't touched another woman since New Year's Eve. Haven't wanted to, and yeah, there've been offers.

Blatant ones.

I'm the king of the fucking Vipers. Bodies are cheap in my world.

I hesitated the last time I had her in my grasp,

and I refuse to make the same mistake now that she's back.

Six fucking months without a word, but it doesn't matter. My body reacts to her like it does to no other.

My dick is painfully hard beneath my tailored pants, and I want her with a need I can barely contain.

Her face is tear-stained, free of makeup, and the loose sundress she has on is crumpled.

Still, she looks beautiful.

There's a glow in her skin that might have something to do with hormones, but I like to think maybe it's the same thing that caused her breath to catch when we exchanged vows.

I don't have a ring for her, but I'll rectify that in the morning.

"I now pronounce you man and wife," Preacher says.

He's a Roman Catholic priest now, but I know him as Preacher. He's a little older than me and was just another punk roaming the streets of Jersey City when I was coming up.

Preacher is over at St. Al's now. But he comes when I call. He still owes me for a little something I helped him out with before he went to seminary school.

"Is that it?" Anna asks him. "Are we married?"

"Yes. You're married now. Um, congratulations, Mrs. Fury. If you ever need anything, the doors at St. Aloysius are always open to you, my child," he says, and looks a little concerned.

Fuck that.

I frown.

"You're dismissed."

Luc nods towards the door and Preacher dips his chin, collects his things and leaves.

I turn to Anna.

My wife.

She's staring at nothing. Her big brown eyes look dull, and a feeling of unease creeps up my spine.

"Let's go," I say, noting it's past midnight and I'm sure she could use some sleep.

"What? Oh."

She gets up and I stare, watching her gracefully lift herself from the chair despite being off balance with her growing belly.

I never thought of pregnant women in sexual terms. But knowing Anna is swollen with my child does something to me.

It stirs something in my loins, and if I didn't know any better, I'd say in my heart as well.

But I'm not a touchy feely guy. The fuck did I know about feelings?

I touch my hand to the small of her back and I guide her out of my office, trusting the biometric security system I have in place to do its job.

"The car is in the back. Need anything else, Boss?" Luc asks.

"No."

I steer Anna down another small hallway. It's easy to miss, and purposely designed that way.

No one uses this exit besides me, Angel, and Luc.

I lift my hand to the scanner and the door unlocks, and I take Anna by her elbow. Carefully, I keep her by my side as we walk to the big SUV.

My driver has the door open, and I glare at him until he steps back.

I don't know why I'm acting like this, but suddenly I feel fiercely possessive of the curvy woman who was now my wife.

I hold her door open for her. Then I let go when I see her contemplating her next move, her small hands on her swollen tummy. Stepping behind her, I lift Anna by her hips onto the seat.

"Thanks," she mutters, and I grunt my response, making a note to have a runner installed.

She's at least a foot shorter than me and in her condition, it's not easy to climb into the truck.

The ride to my place takes about twenty minutes with all the lights and traffic. Anna is quiet for the duration.

When we pull up outside the building I own under my corporation, Viper Enterprises, her mouth drops open.

"You live here?"

"*We* live here," I correct her.

I help her out of the back seat, tuck her hand into the crux of my arm and walk to the private elevator behind the security desk just inside the lobby.

"Good evening, Mr. Fury," Albert, the night watchman greets me.

"Albert, this is my wife, Mrs. Fury. Let everyone know."

"Yes, sir. Congratulations, ma'am."

"Thank you," Anna replies, but I can still feel her surprise.

Situated right on the Hudson River with a spectacular view of Manhattan, I hate to admit I'm a little desensitized to the ritz and glitter of this complex.

Sure, it was designed by top architects and the aesthetic is industrial meets sophisticate. Simplistic, minimal designs using concrete, steel, and glass.

I prefer things black and white, so when I feel Anna shiver beside me I ask her if she's okay.

"Not really. Um, my brother is dead. I'm pregnant. And I'm married to a complete stranger. How on earth can I be okay?" she asks, and she sounds so lost.

I hate it.

And I'm mad for her.

It's not fair to feel this way, I know. But we're not strangers. If we were, she wouldn't be pregnant.

I want to tell her that. To reassure her.

Maybe Anna doesn't know about the snooping I did or the way I planned and arranged to get her in my bed. But that doesn't matter. She is mine now and she will never be alone again.

"Are you hungry?" I change the subject.

"No, thank you. I'm tired. But I have so much to do."

"It's the middle of the night," I say surprised.

"Yeah, but I have to call the hospital and make arrangements for Sammy's remains. Then I have to meet Javi."

"Who?" I ask, tensing at the mention of another man.

"He's the guy Sammy found to manage the bakers," she explains, and I notice her shoulders get stiff when she talks about him.

"I'll deal with it."

I clench my jaw. She won't be talking to this man again. She won't be talking to any man who makes her feel like whatever the fuck that was.

I know it wasn't good. And suddenly, I want to hurt this Javi.

"You don't have to do that," she says and shakes her head.

"Anna," I say her name, the warning clear in my tone. "What's the matter with the bakers? Talk to me."

"They, uh, they're pissed I stayed away so long. They've been trying to bully me into giving them the business for years, and now that I'm back in town, they're giving me an ultimatum. Sign the business over or they walk out."

"Can't you just hire another crew?" he asks.

"Yes, but it takes time to find a crew and a manager and to break them in. In the meantime, I would lose customers we've had for decades."

"Okay. I'll deal with them, too. Now, what else?"

"What do you mean you'll deal with them?"

"Anna, you're dead on your feet. You look like shit."

"Thanks."

"I just mean you need to sleep," I say, biting my tongue. "Look, I don't want you to worry about anything but resting, okay?"

She just stares at me, but she nods. That's a win and I'll take it.

I know Anna doesn't trust me.

Not yet.

But she will.

I give her a very brief tour of the condo, showing her the living room, kitchen, and last, the bedroom.

"Is this my room?" she asks as she steps over the threshold.

"It's our bedroom."

Her shoulders tense again. Only this time it's because of me, and I don't like it.

"B-but—"

"You're my wife and you'll sleep next to me. Every night. In my bed. Understand?"

She looks shocked, but nods. Really, she can't be feeling any more surprised than I am.

Even when we were saying our vows, I had every intention of showing her the guest bedroom at least for tonight. But not now.

Now, I want Anna in my bed. More than ever.

I already know I'm not the wooing kind. Giving orders is more my speed, and she seems to accept my decree.

Or maybe it's just weariness that won out. Either way, I'll take it.

"I don't have any clothes," she whispers.

I frown.

She's right.

"Tomorrow we'll get your stuff from your apartment. You can wear these tonight," I say and grab a pair of soft cotton boxers and a plain t-shirt from my drawer.

Ana moves to the restroom and uses the facilities. She comes out dressed in my clothes and my heart starts to pound steadily.

Now, I've been with all kinds of women. Stunning women with porn star bodies. But none of them could hold a candle to sweet, soft Anna as she walks slowly to my bed wearing my clothes.

Fuck.

That elusive feeling of peace teases the periphery

of my senses. It's a feeling I haven't seen hide nor hair of since the last time I saw her.

It makes no sense. I haven't known her long enough, even if I watched her from afar for weeks before we met.

Somehow, someway I feel a rightness when I am with her.

Like just having her near brings light to the constant darkness that is my life. And knowing she's mine now, well, that does something else to me.

I watch her run her small hand over the covers on my bed with a fierce, rapacious hunger. I know she needs time, so I won't touch her tonight.

Well, I won't touch her much.

I stand and walk to her side of the bed. She freezes in the act of pulling the covers to her waist. Her whiskey-colored eyes flick to mine.

"Is it okay if I sleep on this side?"

"Yeah, Rosebud. Sleep on any side you want."

Then I bend down and cup the back of her head, my fingers gripping her hair, her scalp, and I tilt her towards me. Next, I bring my lips down on hers in a claiming kiss I feel all the way to my soul.

I expected her to duck away or maybe even slap me. But she doesn't. Anna surprises me, lifting her face, angling it the rest of the way all the better to kiss me back.

And I love it. I love feeling her need. Knowing she wants me. That I'm not alone in this crazy pull I feel towards her.

My blood hums in my veins, and my cock is so hard it's almost painful.

I slow the kiss, ending it with a loud, plucking sound, then I press my wife's chest until she lays back her eyes on me while I tuck her in.

"Go to sleep, Wife."

She nods.

"Goodnight, Nico."

Her eyelids droop, closing on their own, and I stay there, my hand on her chest until I feel her breathing even out.

I scrub that same hand over my face as I head to the bathroom and strip. The sight of her clothes in my hamper catches my attention and before I step into the shower, I pick up her cotton panties.

My lips quirk.

They're simple. Little pink bikinis with red hearts sketched across them. I bite my lip and lift them to my face. The scent of my wife's sweet pussy invades my nostrils, and just like that my hard on is back.

I haven't felt that in months. Not since she ran from my bed.

Resisting my urges isn't something I regularly do, so instead of dropping her panties, I take them into the steaming shower with me.

Warm water hits my back and I turn, shoving Anna's panties in my mouth.

Fuck, I wish I was feasting on her cunt. But this will do for now.

Groaning, I cup my aching balls, releasing them to squeeze my dick. And all the while I picture her.

Anna. My wife.

The image of her tear-stained face as she asks for my protection in my office fills my head. The surprised gasp she makes when I order her to marry me is next.

Her submission.

Her swollen belly.

Her whiskey eyes.

And her flower scent.

I stroke faster, squeezing my cock as the first twinges of my orgasm find me.

I think about the way she felt when I fucked her.

How wet her pussy got for me.

How soft and warm she felt.

I can't wait to fuck her again.

She thinks this is only about the baby, but it's not. It's about her.

A primordial wave of possession takes root and I revel in it. I allow it to grow unhindered.

I encourage it to wrap around every rotten inch of my soul as I come, my release splashing across the shower wall.

Anna is mine now. And I'm never letting go.

CHAPTER TEN-ANNA

The bakery is dark when we get there. But that's not unusual. I look around with mixed feelings.

This place is chock full of memories for me. Good times and bad. Times when Dad was stressed out and missing Mom so much, he just fell down the rabbit hole that was drinking and gambling.

I was left to watch out for my little brother and now, in this place, I feel like such a failure.

"I'm sorry," I whisper as I walk behind the counter and touch my fingertips to the old, framed photo of the four of us together.

The picture shows me and Sammy in costumes holding plastic jack-o-lantern buckets, so I know it's Halloween.

I hear the men moving around, but I'm stuck in the past for another minute. Someone opens the door to my office and the protest of the hinges brings my head up.

Nico wanted to be here before the first shift came in. So, it's three in the morning, and I'm tired, but I need to see this through.

Angel is with us. Luc, too. There are a couple of other men, but I think they're just bodyguards or something. They are wearing all black and seem to stand at intentionally spaced intervals.

I don't know what it is about those inked up monsters, but for some reason, I feel safe around them. Maybe it's because they don't look at me for too long.

They don't ask why their king has chosen me. I'm very well aware I'm not the kind of woman a man like Nico Fury would marry.

I haven't found the courage yet to ask how long he plans for us to be wed, but I will.

For now, I'm content to let him take the lead. There is something deeply freeing in placing my life, and the life of our unborn baby, into his large, tattooed hands.

I know I should run screaming. Or object to his

bullying me into marrying him. And sleeping in his bed.

But he's treated me with respect so far, and crazy or not, I feel safe with him.

I feel other things too, but I don't look too closely at that.

It's just hormones.

Mostly.

Well, probably.

I make eye contact with one of the bodyguards, and he quickly turns away. I know it's because of my husband.

I don't think it would be in anyone's best interest to look at Nico Fury's wife too closely. Not because he loves me or anything. More likely, it's because of his reputation.

When I was in Florida, I spent some time scrolling through old newspaper and online articles through my library membership online.

Nico Fury's name comes up quite often in the news. If I believe everything I read, I would have no choice but to think he's insane.

But it's all just speculation. Money laundering, drugs, gambling, real estate schemes.

But no one has ever been able to tie him to any

one crime. Not enough to even garner an arrest warrant, much less convict him.

He's smart. Cunning. And he's so intense.

It's one of the things that makes him so hard to dismiss. When we're together, and his attention is on me, he makes me feel like I'm the only woman in the entire world.

But that's dumb. And I can't afford to be dumb.

I walk into my office and see Nico, Luc, and Angel. It's disorienting. My office is small, and they are so big. They seem to suck out all the air inside the room.

"These your books?" Luc asks.

I nod.

"Can I look at them?" he asks again.

"Sure. Um, an employee has been keeping them for me while I was away. Though I worked some, remotely," I murmur.

Nico is standing beside Luc, his azure gaze on the pages in front of them. I know what he'll see. Red ink. And a lot of it.

"So, this Javi is like the crew boss?" Nico asks.

"Yes. There are two crews. Sammy actually found him when our old guys retired. He hired Javi last year."

"Sammy did?" Nico asks and I swear, I can feel his anger.

His gaze flits to Luc first, and the man makes a gesture I'm sure is code for something, but I have no idea what.

Nico hums a sound of assent. Then he looks at Angel, who simply dips his chin once.

"They've been okay. I mean, there was some trial and error in the beginning with Javi coming in as the crew boss, but some of the guys have been baking bread for us for years," I say, needing to fill the silence.

"They're trying to muscle you out, right?" Angel asks, but his eyes are on his cousin.

"I, well, yeah," I mumble.

His face is calm. Nothing unusual. It's his eyes that give him away. I see his temper flare in their crystalline depths, and it's both wondrous and frightening.

It's like Nico's fury is a living thing. I feel it growing, slithering, contracting and expanding and once again I'm left to wonder if his surname is just a twist of fate or if he chose it.

I should probably ask, but now is not a good time.

Angel hums again. Or maybe it's more of a grunt.

Still, it must have significance because Nico seems to relax once more.

I don't know how I know it, but it is clear these three men just came to some sort of agreement.

And I'm completely in the dark about it.

"Someone's pulling in the back," Angel murmurs, and his voice is so deep it startles me.

He looks so much like Nico, they could be brothers. But I guess being first cousins is close enough. He's bigger though. Taller, too.

"It's them. The bakers. First shift," I reply.

"Let's go," Nico says, but I'm frozen in place.

The baby moves inside my belly, and I close my eyes for a second so I can just feel the tiny life I'm already so in love with.

I didn't know motherhood would hit so hard. Didn't realize I would feel such fierce emotion for my baby.

Maybe it's natural. Maternal instinct. Or maybe it's my desire to have a family, someone of my own, that makes me feel this way.

There's no second guessing for me. I love my baby. And I would do anything to keep him or her safe.

Including marry a stranger.

My chest squeezes, and the baby kicks again. I

open my eyes and Nico is right in front of me. His expression is concerned.

"You need something? Food, water? Maybe you should sit."

I shake my hand, then before I can think better of it, I reach for him. I bite my lip, afraid he'll pull away. But he doesn't.

The king of the Vipers is docile as a kitten as I tug on his big hand and position it over my belly.

"Is that him?" he asks and looks down as our child kicks again.

My gaze is glued to him.

Jesus.

He's so beautiful. A rough man like that probably doesn't get called beautiful often.

But I can't think of another word half as good as that one.

His bone structure is superb. All sharp angles that directly contrast with his plump lips.

They're as soft as they look. I know that first-hand, but still, I wish I could kiss him.

We're married, but he's not mine.

Not like that.

The baby moves again and the corner of his mouth twitches like he might smile. I wish he would.

He doesn't strike me as a man who smiles often,

and for some reason, I want to be the person to make him do just that.

Normally, Nico looks like an avenging angel, all in black, his arm, hand, and neck tattoos visible. But right now he looks stunned, surprised and maybe even happy.

His blue eyes flick to mine, and I swear I am ready to swoon. Those eyes just get me every time.

They're so bright, brilliant really, and I hope like hell our baby inherits them.

Mine aren't bad, but they're just brown. Simple. Plain. And I bite my lip harder.

"Don't," Nico whispers, using his other hand to pull my lip free from my teeth.

His touch lingers on my face before he drags his fingers down to my chin and neck until they drop away, but not before he brushes them over my breast.

The air between us feels charged. Nico's eyes narrow and I suck in a breath, trying not to show how much he affects me.

"Hey, Boss, I'm gonna go talk to the crew," Angel says.

Then he prowls across the room like some sort of big cat.

Nico doesn't so much as look his way.

All his attention is on me, my belly, and I realize he's still touching me with his other hand.

He looks fascinated, and I shiver in response.

"Day after tomorrow we go to the doctor. Gonna get this little one checked out. Little Mama, too," he whispers.

"Okay," I reply.

"Ready to go?" he asks.

"What about the bakers? And the books?"

"Luc and Angel have it."

I nod. Then I step back, forcing his hand to drop.

Truth is, I could use a little break from all his intensity. Nico is an enigma to me.

I suppose I should just feel grateful to him, but that's a shitty way to feel about your baby's father.

I don't want him to see me as some charity case. Even if it's what I am.

If only things were different.

If only he married me because he cared.

He takes my hand and guides me to the door, and I have to work to control my racing pulse.

"Where are we going?"

"To get your clothes," he answers.

I nod again. My apartment is only a few blocks away, but his driver is waiting, and we don't walk there.

"Wait for me," he says when the SUV rolls to a stop outside my building.

I look at it, frowning, wondering what he must think of this place. It's so much worse than his flashy condo.

My door opens, but I'm still stuck somewhere between embarrassment and shame. I hate feeling like that. And the truth is, he has done nothing to warrant it.

It's just me.

All the ugliness I'm feeling is all me.

Shit. Tears prick my eyes, and I suppose I could blame hormones. But that's not all of it.

I know I'm not Nico's type. I'm not even in his league. But he married me, accepted my claim that this baby is his, and just took my word for everything.

I know he's a powerful, smart, cunning, and well-respected man. But I worry I might be bad for him. I might weaken his reputation.

To anyone else, it must look like I tricked him.

"Anna? You okay?" he asks, when I remain glued to my seat.

"I, um, I mean, are you sure about this? It's been a day, Nico. We can get an annulment," I start, needing to offer him a way out.

"No," he growls, pulling me out of the car.

"Look at me," he says, and I obey. "You're my wife now, Anna Fury. The mother of my child. There will be no annulment. No divorce. Not between us. Not ever."

"But what if you fall in love with someone? I don't want to be in your way," I whisper, confessing one of my greatest fears out loud.

"That's not possible," he replies, and my heart constricts.

Does he mean he's incapable of love?

Or that he's already in love with someone else?

Oh my God, does he have a girlfriend? A mistress?

But before I can voice any of those horrible thoughts, Nico takes my hand and turns to the front door of my apartment building.

"Let's get your clothes."

CHAPTER ELEVEN-NICO

I hate her fucking apartment building. It's falling apart and there is no security at all.

The stench of old food lingers in the hallway, beneath that is whatever chemicals the superintendent uses to kill insects and pests.

That can't be good for my Anna or our baby. I frown. Hard.

"Um, I'm not sure if I have boxes," she says, and I shake my head.

"I'll have some people pack it all up for you. Let's just grab some clothes and toiletries. Stuff you need for the next few days," I tell her.

Anna agrees and moves inside, docile as a lamb.

I don't know what she's thinking, or what

happened downstairs to put that stricken look on her face. But I know I don't like not knowing.

I want her to talk to me. To lean on me. Confide in me.

But I suppose that takes time. And I'll give it to her because I wasn't lying downstairs when I said no divorce.

She's not leaving me. Not ever.

This obsession I have with her is no small thing. I might be considered a criminal in the eyes of the law, but I'm honest.

At least, I am about my feelings.

What I feel for Anna is beyond anything I ever felt for anyone.

Hell, I didn't even think I was capable of it. Of love. But when she asked what if I might fall in love, my immediate answer was it's not possible.

Because I already love you.

But I didn't say that part. Not out loud. Not yet.

How could I just drop a bomb like that with no explanation or reasoning?

I have zero experience with love.

Yeah, I've fucked plenty of women. But fucking is not the same as loving. And I haven't touched anyone since I laid eyes on her.

Anna is rummaging around her bedroom. I

watch her through the open door and fuck, she's so beautiful I almost groan out loud.

Instead, I inhale a deep breath. Then I stop moving.

"Do you smell smoke?" I ask.

My phone is in my hand and I'm sending texts to my guys. I start them moving as I grab the duffel bag she's been filling from her bed.

Anna pauses and looks around, sniffing.

"I think I do smell smoke," she says, her eyes wide.

I wait a moment, trying to make sure it's actually fire and not just me overreacting to some asshole burning his toast.

But no. I'm not.

I've smelled fire before, and something is definitely on fire. My hackles were already raised. Have been ever since we left the bakery.

I can't shake the feeling. Now I know why.

Something is fishy about this whole thing. And it all comes back to her dead brother.

Sammy. That fucker.

You shouldn't think ill of the dead, but I don't pander to superstitious bullshit like that.

I'm a bad guy, but Sammy was a fucking leech. My instincts are all fired up. I know he's involved somehow with the trouble Anna has been having with the bakers.

But I can't think about it now, cause if I am right and this building is on fire, we need to leave. Like now.

"Let's go," I say, taking her hand in my free one.

I pull open the door to her apartment, and the air in the hallway is thick with smoke. I can't see two feet in front of me, and the stifling heat is trying to choke me.

The thing about fire is the smoke is black. Not white. Damn near impossible to see through, and even worse to breathe in. I'm not exposing Anna to that.

"Fuck," I growl, pushing us back inside. "Fire escape?"

"Uh, yeah, but it's old."

She points to the window on the far wall of her small eat in kitchen and I pull her towards it.

"Come on," I tell her.

I lift the glass and screen out of the way. Looking out the window, I toss her bag onto it, then I straddle the sill.

"Nico, I'm not sure I can do this."

"Anna, I will keep you and the baby safe. I swear. Do you trust me?"

The look on her face, the hope I see there in her big brown eyes fills me with an overwhelming sense of pride. She places her hand in mine, and I get her out of the window, onto the rickety fire escape.

"Fire department is on their way, Boss," Tommy, my driver, shouts, and I nod.

"Yo, Tommy, catch."

I toss the duffle at him, ignoring Anna's sharp gasp as I move us both to the ladder. Shit. I don't like this.

The old wrought-iron ladder is rusted, and all the paint has chipped away.

I'm not sure it can hold my weight, never mind both of us. But it has to. I won't accept anything else.

"Nico, I feel dizzy," Anna whispers, and I nod.

"It's okay, Rosebud, You just wrap your arms around my neck. Good Girl," I murmur as she steps up to me and does just that.

"Now, hold on," I say, and I lift her up.

Her legs wrap around my waist automatically, and I want to groan. But now isn't the time to get turned on.

Anna's body is fucking perfect. She's got all the curves I desire, just the right amount of meat on her bones, and being pregnant just makes her softer.

She probably thinks she's overweight. In my

experience, most women do, regardless of how they look. But that's bullshit.

I'm a big fucking guy and even holding her like this, I'm able to get us down the ladder, using my legs and arms to create enough space between her back and the rungs.

By now, a crowd has gathered outside the building. It's still super early. Not even four-thirty, but someone pulled the smoke alarm, and it's ringing loudly.

I hear the fire engines pull up and check that Tommy moved the SUV to the corner.

"You can put me down," Anna whispers when we reach the bottom rung, but I don't.

I hold her tighter to me, one hand on her ass as I walk her to the truck. Tommy holds the door open, and I place my wife inside.

"Stay put and buckle up," I tell her just as the fire department arrives.

Flames have engulfed the floor where Anna's apartment is located, I can see them through the window in the stairwell.

Fuck.

Another five minutes and we'd have been truly trapped. I frown. There's no way this is a coincidence, but I'm not going to tell my wife that.

Instead, I walk up to the truck's lieutenant. His eyes widen, and I can see he recognizes me. Most people know who I am. Or if they don't but they have a good sense of self-preservation, they can tell I'm something the first time they meet me.

"Hey," he says, his eyes flash to mine then back to the building.

"Can you tell if it's arson?"

"Will take a little while," he replies, and I nod, taking a business card from my wallet.

"Call me when you know," I say, watching awareness creep into his vision as he reads the name on the card.

I know what it says.

Nico Fury. CEO Viper Enterprises. The Vipers' Den, Jersey City, New Jersey.

Followed by my contact information.

He might not know my name, but he's heard of the Den, and that counts for something. The lieutenant eyes me before he nods sharply.

I walk away from him, back to the SUV where my wife is waiting.

"The condo," I tell Tommy, and he gets in the driver's side while I climb in next to my wife.

Anna already scooted over, making room for me, and I hum in approval. It's the little things that make a person good, and I know she's a good woman.

Even better, she's my woman.

I know she's grieving and maybe a little confused about everything that happened since she came back to town, but all I can think about is fucking her.

Guess that makes me a pig or something.

"So what's going on? Is there really a fire?" she asks.

"Looks like it. But don't worry, I'll replace anything you lose," I explain, hoping to ease some of her worry.

"Oh, I don't care about that stuff, just wow, I mean, you saved me, *us*. You saved us."

"Anna, I wasn't gonna leave you."

"No, I know," she says, and shrugs. "But I'm starting to wonder if maybe you're not some kind of superhero or something."

"I am not a superhero," I scoff.

In fact, I was the total fucking opposite. But her saying that makes me wonder just how fucking innocent my little wife really is. How badly am I tainting her with my presence in her life?

I push the thoughts away.

It doesn't matter because Anna is mine now. And

I'm not giving her up. I'll give her some time to grieve and to get used to the idea of me.

But I don't think I can wait very long to touch her again and I'm not a man used to denying myself.

"Are you okay?" she asks, her soft hand touching my thigh.

I look down at it. My jaw tenses. I want to feel her touch me without any clothes on. I want to see her on her back, spread eagle. I want to hear her beg for my cock.

Am I okay?

No, Rosebud, I'm not fucking okay.

I'm completely obsessed with my wife. And I think I need to hide that from her for a little while at least.

"Nico?"

"I'm fine, Anna."

I'm a liar. I'm not fine.

Part of me wants to go back to the bakery, employ some tactics I'd learned on the job to get Javi to talk.

I know something is wrong with the whole situation. I just don't know what and it's pissing me off.

But another part of me, a newly awakened part, just wants to take Anna home. I want to check her for injury. Make sure she's okay. Then I want to feed her, bathe her, tuck her into bed.

My bed.

I want to kiss her soft lips, pet her smooth skin, and sink into her tight, wet heat. I want to feel her surround me. And I want to make her come on my cock.

Fuck. Yes.

There's a lot I want, but my phone is already buzzing, and I can tell it's from Angel. I have to see to this.

So, I'm gonna take my wife home. Then I'm going to work. Anna yawns, and protective instincts roar to life inside of me. I wrap my arm around her, forcing her to lean on me.

She's stiff at first, clearly shocked. But I just keep my arm there and after a moment, she relaxes. It takes fifteen minutes to get to the condo, and by that time she's asleep.

I sigh. The excitement I feel at holding her sleeping form in my arms is fucking palpable.

Oh yeah, something inside me is changing, and it's all her fault. I hear the question she asked me earlier ring through my brain, and I clench my jaw, staring at her slumber-relaxed face.

"Are you okay?"

I huff a sigh as I lay her gently on the bed, lifting the comforter first so I can pull it over her. Then I kiss her cheek, breathe in her hair, and make a promise to myself to always do right by her.

I won't allow anything else.

"Are you okay?"

Ha. I'm so fucking far from okay.

But I have a job to do. First and foremost, I have to protect Anna and our baby from whatever threat is out there.

It's coming for her. I know it.

I feel it hanging in the air, dense and heavy, like a fog.

I almost feel bad for whoever it is who thinks they can hurt my wife. I smile as I get into the SUV and slam the door.

It's not a good smile. It's the kind of smile a viper gives before he strikes. And it's the only kind of smile I'm used to giving.

I want Anna to love me, but I don't know if she will. I don't know if she can.

Either way, I am hers now. She has my protection and my loyalty.

Anna and our baby are both safe now.

So safe.

If she only knew how fucking safe she is.

CHAPTER TWELVE-NICO

I walk into the Den pissed off and buzzing with energy. The smell of coffee is strong, fresh, and my head snaps to where Maria is pouring a cup.

She holds it out to me.

"Thanks, Maria. Why are you still here?" I ask.

It's not unusual for the bartender to pick up a couple of extra shifts. But closing was three hours ago, and we don't open again till noon.

"I just wanted to make sure you were alright, Boss," she says with a shy smile.

I'm not an idiot. I know something is up with her, and I know she's been flirting with me. I'm just not interested. Never was.

"Look at me," I say.

Her smile disappears the second she makes eye contact. She looks away quickly.

"Any concern for my welfare belongs to my wife and my wife alone. I'm married and I don't cheat, understand?" I tell her, noting her surprise.

"Yes, I-I didn't mean anything, I was just, forget it," she murmurs, laughing nervously.

But she stops before she can outright lie, and I respect her for it.

Maria is a nice girl. Whatever she is looking for, whatever boogeyman she needs to stay hidden from, well I hope she is successful. It just isn't mine to deal with.

"Good. You can keep working if you want. But I have nothing else for you, understand?"

"Yes, Boss. Of course," she says, smiling politely and shaking off whatever all that was.

I take my coffee and walk to my office, not surprised when I see Angel and Luc inside.

Luc is staring at the security screens, and he is not smiling.

Angel's shirt is all wet, and I frown.

"What the fuck happened to you?" I ask.

"Ah, your wife's little friend showed up. Thought I was you. Threw a glass of beer in my face for knocking up her bestie," he says, but he's grinning, and I'm confused.

"Why are you smiling if some woman threw some shit in your face?"

"Cause now she owes me," Angel explains.

"Owes you? You know what, I don't want to know."

And I don't.

"What's the news with the bakers?" I ask.

Angel starts telling me what went down after I left the bakery with Anna. Luc adds what he discovered.

And none of it is good.

"That fucking cocksucker."

I am talking about Anna's brother.

"If he wasn't dead, I'd fucking kill him myself," I growl.

"Yeah, well, he did sell you a night with his sister to clear up his debts," Angel states what all of us already know.

But it makes me fucking mad.

"Easy, Boss," he grits, and I look down to see I have my hands wrapped around his throat.

"Alright, let's make a plan," I say and sit back down in my chair.

I'm not going to talk about my reaction to his statement. I don't really want to think about how I tricked Anna into my bed.

She is there now, and that's all that matters.

CHAPTER THIRTEEN-ANNA

I wander through the condo after I wake up alone.

Again.

An entire week has passed, and I barely see Nico. I'm so lonely, but I'm healthy and that's a plus.

There's a housekeeper who comes every other day. She's older, friendly, and I like her very much.

But she is there to work, not to be my friend, and I hate taking up her time when I know she has her own family to go home to.

The doctor said everything looked great. All my tests were excellent. The baby is healthy, and we even saw him on the tiny little screen when they did the ultrasound.

It's confirmed. We are having a boy.

Nico looked so proud when they told us. Of course, I teared up. Being pregnant was like being a giant walking hormone.

He didn't seem to mind, though. Nico just wrapped his arms around me and held me tight against his hard, powerful body. He kissed my head, whispering words of praise I never expected, but really needed to hear.

We buried Sammy's ashes in the plot where our parents were laid to rest. It wasn't a real funeral. Just a short service.

Private. Small. Tasteful.

Exactly the kind of thing I could handle right now.

Sammy didn't have friends. He'd spent the little time he had on earth feeding the monster that was his addiction.

So, it was just me, Giselle, Nico, Luc, and Angel.

I wept like a broken thing. Hiccupping and sobbing until Nico picked me up and carried me out of there.

He held me the whole ride home and put me to bed. Him carrying me was becoming a thing, and normally I'd be freaking out.

I mean, I'm a big girl. But Nico was bigger than

me. Clearly, he could pick my chubby ass up like I was a sack of potatoes and not think twice about it.

I think I'm actually getting used to it. And I'd be lying if I said I didn't like it. Usually, he left me in the bed to sleep alone. But not that day.

Nico crawled in under the covers with me, and he just held me in silence.

It was exactly what I needed at the time. But I feel so confused now. I don't know what to make of him.

This man. My husband.

Walking to the large closet I bite my lip and look through the dozens of new clothes Nico had me order.

Smoke and water damage ruined pretty much everything I had in my old place. I couldn't walk around naked, so I gave in without a fight.

Besides, my belly is only getting bigger. And maternity clothes were cute as fuck.

July is just so fucking hot and sitting in the penthouse, no matter how luxurious is still just sitting around. I'm uncomfortable. I need movement.

The idea of going out alone isn't really appealing, especially since the fire department confirmed arson. I mean, I don't know who'd actually want to hurt me, but I can't risk it.

So, until I broach the subject with Nico, I'll stay put.

It's a little better now that I found Nico's rooftop swimming pool. I mean, his condo is technically the penthouse, but I didn't know that meant he owned the roof amenities too.

I go to check in with Arnold, using the intercom on the wall.

He's security, but his position is outside the front door. Nico won't have anyone in the house while I'm here alone, and I appreciate that.

"I'm going swimming, Arnold," I tell him.

"Roger that, Mrs. Fury. Want me to open the roof?"

"Yes, please."

"You got it, Ma'am."

I chuckle at him calling me ma'am. Hands on my back, I walk up the spiral staircase, a towel slung over my arm.

It's only like nine stairs to the door leading to the pool, but I take them slowly. Ever since I got pregnant my equilibrium has been completely off.

I push the door open and smile as the ceiling retracts, allowing fresh air to swirl about, and sunshine to rain down on half of the crystal clear pool.

My cell phone chimes. I pluck it from the pocket

of the robe I'm wearing and I read a message from Giselle.

GISELLE

So, what does a girl wear when going to the Vipers' Den?

ANNA

What the what now? Why are you going there?

GISELLE

Got into some trouble. See, I thought I was sticking up for your preggo ass and I kinda sorta showed up the other day and threw a glass of beer into some huge man's face I thought was Nico.

I laugh out loud. So hard, I almost freaking pee. I could just picture my bestie, her green eyes flashing and curly black hair bouncing as she goes toe to toe with Angel fucking Fury.

ANNA

Please tell me you didn't sell yourself to my husband's cousin.

GISELLE

OMG. Get a grip. You're the only Slutty McSlutterstein around these parts, Girl.

I don't answer. I know she's trying to be funny, but something about it just makes me sad.

GISELLE

Anna. ANNA! God, I am sorry. I didn't mean to say that. I'm not judging you. anyway, how is it?

ANNA

How's what? Being a slut? I wouldn't know. I haven't had sex in six months.

I tell her honestly, and now I'm crying.

Like a moron.

What kind of person gets sad because the man who basically forced her into marriage when he finds out he accidentally knocked her up after their one night stand, which coincidentally, he also instigated because her brother owed him money, won't have sex with her?

I am so screwed up.

GISELLE

Anna, I am sorry. I didn't mean it. Are you okay? Please answer me.

But I don't.

Giselle and I have known each other forever.

She's like my sister. So, she knows my moods. And after ten minutes of her trying to call me, she stops.

She knows I'll call her back when I'm feeling less salty. Which could be an hour or a day or even a week. It all depends.

Sighing, I turn my phone off and tug on the belt to my terrycloth robe. I'm naked beneath it, but it's not like I have anything to worry about.

Nico isn't home. I'm all alone. And even though I bought a couple of maternity bathing suits, I don't like how they feel.

I hate clingy fabric to begin with. But with this baby belly, it's so much worse.

The water is warm, but cool enough to be refreshing in all the cloying heat. I sigh as I sink down to my shoulders. After a few minutes, I lie back, just allowing my body's natural buoyancy to carry me.

The sound of water rushes in my ears as I float lazily. No raft or noodle, just me. It's just something I always liked to do. I watch the clouds floating by and allow my mind to drift. I close them and focus on breathing. My body feels so light, suspended in the water. And I relax.

Something slams, *the door maybe,* and I startle,

opening my eyes to find a pair of brilliant, glowing blue eyes staring back at me.

It's Nico. And he is fucking furious.

CHAPTER FOURTEEN-NICO

Married for over a week and I have the worst fucking case of blue balls in history.

Every fucking night I stay out late. Going over business deals and just biding my fucking time. I know if I go home, I'll take her. I'll be buried inside her sweet heat so fucking fast just cause she's there and she's mine.

But I want more from Anna than her body. And I don't want to rush her.

I just had Angel update all my home security, and I notice something funny when I go to check that everything is running smoothly.

"Angel!" I roar.

"What's up?" my cousin asks as he comes storming into my office.

"Who the fuck is this clown?" I growl, turning my monitor towards him.

"Doesn't matter. He's dead," my cousin answers.

It's a good answer.

I stand up and head for the door. My blood is fucking boiling. We're fifteen minutes away from my condo, and I can hardly wait.

"I fucking vetted him."

This is Angel's apology. I know he's angry. Possibly as angry as I am.

But maybe not quite.

"Not close enough," I snap.

I don't normally wear a holster in the office, and the only gun on me is a Glock 45 I have tucked into the back of my pants. I don't want to shoot him, though.

This is a personal offense, and it requires something more up close and confrontational than a bullet to the brain.

"I'll take care of this, Nico," Angel promises, but I shake my head.

"No. I'll take care of this. You clean it up and you'll be on guard duty till I approve someone else," I snarl, and he nods.

Cleaning isn't for a man in his position. But then

again, he's the one responsible for this fuck up and this is how he'll pay for it.

The inside of the SUV is frigid, just how I fucking like it and Tommy is speeding, taking side streets and alleys while I plan exactly what I'm going to do to the motherfucker who's working as my wife's security today.

I close my eyes and let rage fill me.

About seventeen minutes later, the elevator doors open, and that motherfucker stumbles, trying to zip up his pants.

His hands go for the mouse on his computer monitor, like he thinks I don't know he's been sitting here, jerking off, while watching my wife swim in her pool.

The affront this man has done to me fuels my already overblown need for revenge.

"Boss! No, no, pleas—"

But that's as far as he gets. I grab a pen from the cup on the small security desk right outside my condo and ram it into his throat.

I stab him again. And again. He gurgles. His hands clutch my shoulders, but I don't stop.

I keep stabbing, wiggling the pen around trying to pierce every vein I can. Then I use the writing implement to pop his eyeballs out of his fucking head. Next, I cram them down his useless throat.

The pen really is mightier than the sword. I grin before I look at the man's limp form. Then I frown.

"Motherfucker," I snarl, and spit on his fucking face before letting him drop to the floor.

"Put him with the rest," I tell Angel, and he's already in action.

Angel is nothing if not prepared. He places the case he brought with him onto the marble floor. The first thing he removes is a thick black body bag.

I leave him to it and walk inside the condo. I'm still seething. And there's only one thing that'll calm the beast raging inside me.

I roll my neck, hunting my wife through the silent condo. Normally, I walk slowly through the space, taking in all the subtle differences having a woman there has made.

Anna doesn't do anything too big. Nothing she thinks might bother me, and I plan to cure her of that misunderstanding.

Truth is, I want her to mark this place. I want her to claim it, *to claim me*, as her own. I can't wait to see what happens when she does.

I catch a glimpse of my face in the mirror, and I grunt. Blood is liberally splattered over my skin, and

I tear off my shirt, using it to wipe the crimson wetness from my face.

It's drying out now and I feel it on my hands, but I can't take the time necessary to wash it off. I have to see her.

I jog up the stairs to the pool area and open the door, stopping when I find her floating in the pool.

But it's not like my gorgeous wife is simply swimming. No, she's butt ass fucking naked and her luscious body is drifting on top of the pool.

Her eyes are closed, and she looks even more relaxed than when she's sleeping.

Rivulets of water sluice over her form, cascading between her breasts and pooling at the cropped curls covering the apex of her thighs. With her belly six months swollen with our baby, she's even fucking hotter.

And I am done waiting.

CHAPTER FIFTEEN-ANNA

I stand up in the water, bringing my hands up to cover my nudity. But I'm too slow. Or Nico is just really fast.

He's kicked off his shoes already. The water splashes as he jumps in landing right in front of me.

"Nico? W-what—"

But that's all I have time to utter. He's closing the distance, slamming his mouth to mine, and God help me, I love it.

"I tried to give you time. But I'm not waiting anymore. You're mine Anna, and I'm gonna fuck you like you're mine," Nico says.

His voice is gravelly and his eyes blazing, and more than anything, I hope he's telling the truth.

I know I should refuse him. I should say no. But I

don't want to. In fact, I'm fairly certain I want to be his.

My body is humming, feeling alive for the first time in months. I want him to touch me. I'm desperate for him.

"Fuck. Anna, you're so wet," he says into my mouth, and I swallow his words whole.

He has two fingers buried inside my pussy and his other hand on my ass holding me tightly to him as he ravages my mouth.

Nico's kiss is just as unbridled and wild as he is. His tongue is so long and firm, snaking into my mouth, leaving no part untouched.

I moan and suck on it, loving the way he tastes. I don't know if it's something he eats, a candy or a drink, but to me, Nico tastes like cayenne and honey.

Hot and sweet and so fucking sexy.

I open my eyes and notice red dots on his neck. But the water washes them away, and he's touching me again, and I forget all about them.

"You want me just as much as I want you. Don't you, Rosebud? Look how fucking needy you are, squeezing my fingers so damn tight."

I nod. I am so needy. And it's his fault.

He's the one who dies this to me. No one ever

made me feel like Nico did. It's like he knows exactly where to touch me and how.

The filthy words he whispers while he walks me to one of the stools at the swim up bar on this side of the pool has me moaning. I'm trapped inside the steel bands of his embrace and there is nowhere else on earth I want to be.

The past six months I dreamed of this, of him, but the reality is so much better. Nico isn't some silent participant. He doesn't just take his pleasure and leave me wanting.

No, he talks. And he touches. He commands. And he moans. He owns me with his body. And I don't think there is anything sexier than when he's telling me how hard he is for me.

"Feel my dick? I'm so hard and ready. All for you, Rosebud. Christ, I was dying here without you."

I gasp as he takes my hand and forces it onto his thick shaft. I squeeze it. Moaning at both the feel of his dick in my hand, and the loss of his fingers as he pulls them from my aching pussy.

"Show me how much you want me, Wife. Suck my dick with your hot little slit."

Nico plops me down on the stool and reaches between us. And that's when I feel it.

When I feel him.

The big, broad head of his thick cock presses against my entrance, and I moan long and loud at the sudden invasion.

"Take it, Rosebud. Take me," he groans and wraps one hand around my throat.

That act alone is enough to make my pussy clench. The fact he's filling me just makes it that much better.

He's so big. So strong. And he is everywhere.

Touching me. Kissing me. Praising me for taking him so deep.

"Jesus Christ. You feel so fucking good. That's it, Good Girl," he grits out when my pussy spasms, squeezing him tightly.

"Nico," I whimper, needing him to move.

"This pussy was made for me, Rosebud. It's fucking mine. Tell me."

"Yours, Nico. All yours. Please."

I should be embarrassed by my reaction to him, by how quickly I turn into a submissive, needy, whiny little thing.

But that's just it.

I'm not embarrassed by my need for him. I feel empowered by it. I feel sexy and wanton. And for the first time in my life, I feel desired.

My breasts are squashed against his chest. And I

wrap my legs around him tighter. I cling to him, loving the delicious friction he's creating between our bodies, but needing more.

His mouth licks into mine, and he's so hot. Spicy and sweet. He doesn't let me up for air. He just kisses me, and kisses me, his thick dick twitching inside my channel. But he's so still. And it's driving me mad.

I'm close. One touch, one flex of his hips, and I'll explode.

My fingers try to hold on to his huge shoulders, but his muscles are flexing beneath my hands, slippery with water, making it impossible for me to maintain my grip.

I try to rock my hips, but he holds me still. Kisses me the whole while. But not letting me move.

"You taste like fucking cherries. And sunshine. Goddam delicious."

I whimper. He slides his hand between us. I feel his thumb press against my swollen clit, and I moan.

It's agonizing.

It's amazing.

He circles it slowly, building my pleasure, but all I want is for him to move that big dick inside me. But he won't. And I might just fucking hate him for that.

"Such a good wife. So needy for me. Come on, Wife. Tell me what you need."

I can't take anymore.

I never want him to stop.

"Please. Nico," I beg.

"Please what?"

"Move. I need you to move," I finally tell him.

"You want me to move? What do you want me to move?"

"Your thing. Your c-cock. I need you to move," I whispered.

"I like it when you say cock, Rosebud," he moans, licking into my mouth.

He rocks a little. It's not enough. But it feels good. And I moan into his mouth.

"Come for me first. I need you to come for me right here, Rosebud, then I'll move. I'll take you to the bed and I'll fuck you proper," he tells me, and that does it.

"Gimme a taste of all that pleasure, Baby. Come. For. Me."

He presses harder, accentuating every word by squeezing my tight little nubbin.

By the time he says *me*, I'm already coming.

CHAPTER SIXTEEN-NICO

I didn't make it to our bed.

Far as I got was one of the outdoor sofas that sat around the pool deck. With a voice command, I close the roof, wanting more privacy. Wanting to be alone with my wife.

I already locked down the security feed right after I found that motherfucker peeping on my Anna. I'd talk to her later about swimming in the nude without me here.

Right now, I'm beyond words. All I want is to bury my dick inside her hot cunt. So, I sit down with Anna in my arms and on my lap.

We're both dripping wet, but I don't fucking care. I grab her by the insides of her soft, juicy thighs and I lift her up.

"Hold my cock," I grunt, and she does, placing it at her entrance.

Then I drop her, impaling on my dick, and she takes over.

My wife is so fucking hot. She bounces up and down on my dick, and I am mesmerized. I don't know where to look.

Should I stare at her glorious tits as they jiggle with every move?

Or the ecstatic expression on her face, lips parted, eyes at half mast, cheeks flush?

Or the sight of her sweet pussy moving up and down on my cock like she was born to do just that?

Fuck.

There is no other choice, I take it all in.

I take her all in.

Every bit of her. And I make it a part of me.

"Anna," I groan her name, taking control by grabbing her hips.

Up. Down. Again and again. I relish every trembling move, every vibration and flutter that tells me just how close she is to coming all over me.

I can't wait. I need her. I need all of her.

"Jesus, Rosebud. Hear that. Listen to how wet your pussy is for me," I say, and the slapping sounds of our bodies fill my ears, and they're sweeter than any symphony.

"Tell me I can have you whenever I want," I say, pulling her down and grinding her into me.

I have my hand around her throat, and I force her eyes to mine.

"Y-yes," she whispers, eyes glassy with unfinished passion.

She looks drunk. Or high. And I like that. I like that she's drunk on my dick.

So eager to please, so willing to be mine. Her total submission is at my fingertips, and it's what I want.

Well, it's a start.

"No more distance. This starts our marriage. Right here. Right now."

She nods.

I rock harder, thrusting my hips up.

"You're mine, Anna. No one else gets to see you, hear you, or touch you."

"Who? What are you?"

I shake my head.

"No one else. Tell me you understand."

"No one else," she says, nodding her head in agreement.

"Good, cause if anyone even tries, I'll kill them," I growl.

And instead of slapping me or pushing me away, horrified by my own dark admission, Anna proves how perfect she is for me.

She starts to come. Her pussy tightens. Her eyes roll back, and her mouth opens on a long moan.

I don't hold back.

I follow her into sweet oblivion. I slam my mouth to hers, claiming her lips, and I come harder than ever before.

After a few moments, when I can move again, I carry my sweet wife to the shower beside the pool and rinse us both off. Then, because she winced a little, I carry her back to the pool.

"What are you doing?" she asks.

"Well, I figure you were in here cause it relieves some of the pressure you feel from the baby," I say, and she nods, biting her lip.

She looks so damn cute when she does that.

"What are you doing home so early?" she asks.

My eyebrows raise.

"Would you rather I come home late?"

"No! I mean, no, I like having you home," she replies, and her cheeks turn pink.

Fucking adorable.

"I like being home, too."

"Here, you were floating before, right? How does

this feel?" I ask, moving to stand behind her.

I tuck my arms around her, supporting her weight on my chest while the rest of her just floats freely. Anna smiles, and my heart almost stops beating.

Goddamn.

I've never been the cause of anyone's smiles.

Screams? Sure. But not smiles. Not like hers.

The woman has a smile that knocked the sun right out of the sky. I like making her smile. I want to do it more.

Her palms press down on the tops of my hands, and I think she's going to push me away, but she doesn't.

She is clinging to me. To me. Like I am something worthy of her.

Fuck, I want to be.

I am humbled. I am in awe. And suddenly, I have a new addiction.

Fucking Anna is an addiction I know I have. I mean, for months before I saw her in person, I obsessed over her. Then I touched her, and I was ruined for anyone else.

I just can't get enough of her. The taste of Anna. The sound of her. Goddamn, her moans call to me. I replay them in my mind.

And I imagine her tight, sweet heat squeezing me. My fingers flex against her flesh, and she sighs and nuzzles my arm with her face.

The pool water is at a comfortable temperature. Cooling from all the stifling heat, but not cold.

But I don't care about the water. I only care about her. How she feels in my arms as I rock with her in the pool. I have a natural slat filter, so I know there aren't any chemicals that could harm her or the baby.

"This is nice," I say, and she hums her agreement.

Truthfully, it's as close to relaxing as a guy like me can get. Anna does that for me. She gives me peace.

This woman is everything. She's the home I didn't know I needed. That missing piece of me I wasn't sure I'd ever find.

But I did find her. Here she is, and I need her, and I want her. I covet her and our baby boy. She makes me want to be better for the both of them.

She makes me want a life beyond the dark. It's a dream I have had seldom in my life. But I have had it.

Only, with her, it doesn't feel so far away. With her, it feels possible.

"What are you thinking about so loud over

there?" she asks, and I can see by the glint in her whiskey eyes that she's teasing me.

"I'm thinking I got everything I want right here," I tell her, holding her gaze.

I see surprise, shock even, then something else. Something rare and beautiful. I see hope, and my chest feels tight.

"What is it, Rosebud?"

"Nothing, I mean, well, I just wasn't sure if this was something you wanted or something I forced on you."

Forced on me? Is she serious?

Does this sweet beauty feel guilty?

Does she think she tricked me into marrying her or something?

Fuck me.

That's exactly what she thinks. I can see it on her face.

"Anna," I say, helping her stand and turning her around to face me.

I grip the base of her neck with one hand and hold her cheek with the other hand.

"You are all I ever wanted," I admit.

"W-what are you talking about? I only met you because of Sammy's debt to you," she whispers her brother's name.

"That's true, but not how you think. You see," I say, daring to tell her something.

Something real.

"I only allowed Sammy to ring up a bill so I could have you."

"What?"

"I'm a powerful man, Anna. I run a tight organization," I say, even though I'm still feeling raw about that fucking sleazy security guard who watched my wife swim in the nude.

"I don't lend money without doing research. Sam had nothing to offer as collateral. But I saw a picture of you, and I wanted you."

"Y-you tricked me? My brother? You let him gamble just so you could fuck me?" she says, and fuck, I see devastation in her eyes.

"No. Well, yes. But not how you think. Not so I could fuck you once and let you go. If you hadn't run, I wouldn't have been able to stay away." I admit.

She doesn't know the half of it. The way I stalked her. My invasion of her privacy. And I won't tell her any of that.

"You wouldn't have been able to stay away? What are you talking about? Why?" she asks, and I can see she is serious.

Fuck.

Doesn't she know?

"What do you need me to say, Anna? That I want you. I do. That I'd do anything to keep you? That I'd fucking kill for you? Cause I will," I say, and my chest is heaving.

"Nico—"

I can't let her finish because I don't know what she is going to say. And it scares me.

Me.

I'm the fucking boogeyman, and this little slip of a girl scares me half to death.

"I'm not good with words. I didn't go to college. I'm no fucking Shakespeare, but I'll treat you good. And I'll protect you with my life."

There it is. I spell it out for her. And now I'm frozen.

Half-frightened out of my mind that she'll shove me away and tell me to get lost.

I won't do it even if she does.

It's not even a question.

But if she says that to me, *if she rejects me*, I'm not sure I won't lose my fucking mind and I already killed one man today.

My beautiful wife looks down, and I have to relax my hand to allow the movement.

I do. And I wait.

Finally, she lifts her pretty face to mine, and her eyes are glittering with unshed tears.

"I don't need you to give me poetry, Nico. I just need you," she says.

For the first time, my wife lifts her face to mine, her tiny hands around my tattooed neck, and she pulls me to her for a kiss.

And it's everything.

I need Anna to want me like this.

To cling to me. To know she can come to me for anything.

For support.

For pleasure.

For protection.

I just want to keep her safe, to make her feel good. To keep her. Period.

"You ready for a shower now?" I ask, and she nods.

Hugging me to her one more time.

Fuck.

She feels so good. So soft and warm.

I hold her hand and help her out of the pool. I walk slowly, carefully so she doesn't slip on the tiles.

"You have nice hands," she murmurs, tracing the skull tattoo on my right one.

"You like my hands?" I ask as I hold her robe

open for her.

She slides her arms into it and I wonder what she would say if I told her I murdered our security guard with those same hands just a little while ago.

Would she hate me?

Would she regret letting me touch her?

I really don't know. But I can't regret my actions.

Anna is mine, and an insult to her is one to me. I'll let neither go unpunished. Everyone will get the message. They'll all know.

My wife is not to be fucked with.

CHAPTER SEVENTEEN-ANNA

I stare at my phone and roll my eyes, placing it face down on the kitchen table. Nico made me hard boiled eggs and toast before he left to meet with his accountant, but he's coming to pick me up for dinner later.

I need an outing. Seriously, I'm starting to grow roots.

Sure, the condo is awesome. And Nico even told me I could hire a decorator to change anything I want.

But really, I'm fine with the neutral walls, warm

wood floors, polished marble bathrooms, and floor to ceiling windows.

Most of the furniture is decidedly masculine, but a little accessorizing can help with that.

I already ordered like three dozen throw pillows and a variety of materials with different textures and colors so I can sew cases for them.

I have a secret passion for interior design and sewing. I'm always looking up projects and plotting out things to work on.

Like the jewel-toned blue quilt I just finished for our king-sized bed. I spent about thirty hours on it. I ordered the material online and found a handy little sewing machine in the closet that the housekeeper uses sometimes.

Anyway, whenever he isn't home. I work on things for the house. I ordered sheets to match, replacing all the old ones in our bedroom.

Our bedroom.

Warmth seeps into my veins as I bite down on a piece of perfectly buttered rye toast. I place one hand on my belly, and I chew slowly.

There's no escaping the fact I am all in this. Conventional or not, I am really liking married life.

My phone chimes again.

GISELLE

Pleeeeeeeaaaaaaaasssssssssseeeeeee. I need to talk to you. This thing with Angel is making me crazy. I'm sorry for judging you. Heeeellllllllllllpppppppppppp. I'm an asshole. You can call me a bitch. And I'll let you blow a raspberry in my face. Just please please please please please please please please.

I can't take it anymore. I hit call and connect to video.

"Oh my God, does this mean you forgive me?"

"No heifer, it means you can come over and grovel and maybe I'll let you swim in my rooftop pool with me," I say.

"You bitch, you have a pool now?"

"Uh huh. I do."

"Are those boiled eggs? You never make those right! The shell always sticks," she says suspiciously.

"I didn't make them. Nico made them for me."

"No, he did not!"

"Yes. He did. He cooks all the time. Actually, I think he's kind of obsessed with what I eat, and um, feeding me."

Now that I think about it, he is rather insistent about it. Every night since the day we made our marriage real in the swimming pool, which is also the last day I ever saw our old security guard, Nico's been coming home early and cooking for me.

We eat together. We talk. Watch TV. We swim.

But of course, swimming leads to other things.

Not that I'm complaining. I completely love doing *other things* with Nico. But I also miss Giselle.

Six months apart is nothing, I mean she left for college and our friendship survived. I'm still kinda pissed at her insinuating I'm some sort of actual slut when we both know that's not true.

But I could use a friend. Someone to help me sift through the feelings I'm having.

"Just get your ass over here," I say, and she squeals, making me drop the phone.

It will take her at least twenty minutes to get here, so I go take a shower and I pull on a tank top and shorts.

The temperature is set at 65 degrees, but being pregnant makes me feel constantly warm. I hear a commotion in the hallway, and I walk to the door.

When I open it, I'm greeted with a sight I wouldn't have expected in a million years.

Angel Fury has his arms wrapped around Giselle, and he's kissing the hell out of her. Her eyes look glazed over when he finally lifts his head.

"Get inside, *Koukla*," he grunts, swatting her ass before dipping his chin at me.

Giselle blinks slowly. Then she walks right towards me, her eyes wide and her lower lip between her teeth.

I have so many questions.

CHAPTER EIGHTEEN-NICO

I frown as my phone buzzes, but I don't ignore it.

Typically, I do not allow interruptions when I'm in business meetings, but ever since Anna came into my life, I feel a compulsion to be available at all times.

I mean, fuck, if she needed me and I was too busy to answer, I'd never forgive myself.

I grab my phone and glance at it, reading the name of the person texting me. It's Angel with an update.

Seems my wife invited a friend over today. A female friend, so that makes it okay, but still, I need to have a talk with her about that.

Of course, Anna can have anyone she wants over,

but she should tell me first so I can clear it with security.

Angel's got something going on with that Giselle woman, Anna's best friend, so he allowed her to come up the elevator. But if he wasn't still on guard dog duty, she'd never have passed clearance.

"Mr. Fury?" my realtor says my name, and I turn my gaze to him.

He can't hold it very long. So, he drops his eyes and taps the document he wants me to look at.

It's a prospectus for a new development down the shore. One of those retirement complexes for people over fifty places, but I think I'll pass.

For some reason, I'm more interested in the project to build low income housing right here in Jersey City. Sure, the government has plenty of spots, but those buildings are shit holes.

Overrun with violence, drugs, and ill health.

People need a better place to start. Families need a place to live where they feel safe.

Maybe I'm feeling sentimental because my own son is growing inside my wife at this very moment, and both of them mean the world to me.

"I want to invest in the project on Kearny Avenue," I tell him and stand up.

I'm done with this meeting.

"But Mr. Fury," he starts, and I spin on my heel.

"Did I stutter, Borello?"

"No, sir," he mutters.

"Good."

I leave, ready to be done with the day, so I can take my wife to dinner. But I'm not finished yet. I have an appointment to visit some guys at city hall.

Fucking politicians and city employees. Every single one of them has their hand out, and yet, they call me the gangster. What a fucking joke.

But it's the cost of doing business and Viper Enterprises has earned its place in the hierarchy of moguls and corporations working the system.

Everyone plays their part, I just play mine better.

I might not have gone to college, but I know how the world works and I'm not stupid. Growing up running wild in the city streets meant I listened, and I learned.

Some lessons were harder than others. I look at one of the many scars I have, this one on my right forearm, and I exhale slowly.

My son will not learn lessons like that. He will be strong, yes. But he will also be loved. And that's not something I have a lot of experience with, but I have a feeling it will make all the difference.

My Anna knows love. The affection she feels for

our baby is clear on her sweet face whenever I catch her touching her stomach or just daydreaming about him.

I know her life hasn't been easy. She's worked hard, and mostly alone, for way more of her life than most people her age. I know she's going to be thirty-three in December.

That makes her seven years younger than me. I'll be forty a week before her birthday.

I can't believe I lived that long. But now that I have her, now that she's given me a family, I'm determined to double my years.

Besides, only the good die young and I'm not that.

Nah. That's a fucking lie.

My Anna is good, and I refuse to even think for a second she might leave this world before I do.

It hits me then.

I love her.

Fuck.

I can't breathe. I know I care. That I am obsessed. But love?

Double fuck.

All the crazy emotions I've been feeling for this woman for more than half a year now all add up to one thing. I am completely besotted. Head over fucking heels.

I love her.

And there is something about acknowledging my love for her that makes my heart beat double time and sets my dark soul to soaring.

I have to tell her. There's no excuse for keeping it a secret. I want to tell her right now, but I think it needs to be face to face.

I sigh and scrub my hand over my face, running my palm over my short beard.

What will her reaction be?

I don't pretend I deserve her love. I mean, I know I don't. I basically bullied her into marrying me after I knocked her up and failed to track her down.

Okay, I didn't know she was pregnant, but still. I knew I wanted her, and I let her get away. I thought I was being merciful, keeping her out of my fucked up life.

But I see now that I was just justifying my own fucking cowardice. I admit it now, in the car, to myself, I was afraid Anna would reject me.

The streets blur as I think about how that might have gone down. If Anna told me no. If she refused me.

What would I have done?

I shake my head. It's best not to think about it. Because Anna didn't reject me. She didn't turn me down.

Fuck.

When I think of how readily my sweet Rosebud submits to me every single time I touch her, my cock starts to harden, and I have to work to get it to back the fuck down.

I'm not going into a meeting with some greasy fucking councilman sporting a chubby.

"Traffic ahead. Looks like an accident," Tommy, my driver, says.

"Take the turn ahead. Cut around," I tell him.

I exhale again. My nerves are all fired up, and I don't want to be here. I want to be home.

With her.

Sometimes I feel like two sides of a coin. One side is the king of the Vipers. The ruler of a criminal organization that commands respect in the tri-state area.

The other side is just me.

Nico Fury. The man.

I think of Anna as we take a side street. My driver knows where to go, and with the accident behind us, I don't need to pay attention.

I think of her pretty face and her sweet, soft

body. The way she moaned my name when I woke her up this morning with my face between her thighs.

She's so goddamn beautiful. So fucking delicious.

I can't get enough of her.

But even as I remember all the dirty, sexy things we did just hours ago, I'm alert. My senses are working, and my body is attuned to my surroundings.

I'm always fucking aware of my surroundings. I have to be.

It's how I survived this long. I keep myself loose, my hands rest on my thighs, and I look at my left one in particular.

Hmm.

That reminds me, I have something to do before I go to this next meeting.

"Take the next left. We're making a pit stop at Trapp's," I tell my driver, and he nods.

"I can't believe it. I mean, *you* and *Angel*," I whisper, completely shocked.

"Yeah, well, it was a shock to me, too. But obviously, it's not serious. I mean, I just owed him because of the whole beer in his face incident," she mumbles.

I start to giggle. I can't help it. It turns into a fit of full belly laughter, and I snort. I slap my hand over my mouth.

"Oh my God, Anna! Are you snorting at me?"

Giselle shakes her head, but I can tell she wants to laugh, too.

"Oh, Sisi, you should see your face," I say between laughing and sucking in gulps of air.

I make us a pot of herbal tea, place some cookies

on a plate for us to share, and we talk about Sammy. It's still difficult to think of my little brother as dead, but I know it will get easier with time. At least, I hope it will.

"How are you holding up?" Giselle asks.

"It's hard, you know. Sammy was a lot, but he was still my brother," I say tearfully.

She hands me a napkin and moves her chair closer so she can wrap her arm around me.

"You took such good care of him, Anna. Way better than your dad, and I'm sorry. I know you don't like it when I judge people, but he checked out on the two of you long before you were even an adult. Sammy had plenty of good examples from you, but he made his own decisions."

"I know, but he died so horribly," I say, remembering the way he'd crawled to the curb, beaten and bloody the first night I was back from Florida.

"Yes, he did. And I am sorry for that. For him and you, but Anna, there was nothing you could do. I mean, I know you are happy now. I can see it on your face. But I can't pretend to not know how you got here. Sammy sold you to pay his debt. And that's fucked up. Mourn your brother, but don't fool yourself into thinking he was some kind of saint," she says, and I know she's right.

Her words sound cold, but she's just practical. And it is exactly what I needed to hear. I'm still carrying so much guilt for Sammy's death, it's like an invisible weight pressing down on me.

This talk helps. The weight is still there, but not like before. I thank Giselle and I hug her, and we both wind up crying in our tea.

We spend the rest of the afternoon swimming in the pool. Then we shower and paint our toenails. I show her the guest room and she teases me about moving in.

I'm having so much fun. Being with Giselle is both nostalgic and refreshing. It feels like the sleep-overs we used to have when we were younger.

"Wow, this is amazing," she says, entering the huge walk-in closet that's actually bigger than my old bedroom.

I bite my lip as Giselle takes in the racks of designer clothes. Not all of them are maternity, and we spend some time playing an adult version of dress up.

"Are you sure I can borrow this?" she says, eying the price tag on the sexy little black dress she's tried on.

We're both curvy girls, though she's taller and her

breasts are bigger than mine. But we basically wear the same size.

The dress is shorter on her than it would be on me, but she fills out to perfection.

"Um, yeah. You look hot," I tell her, and do a spin in the short chocolate brown swing dress I slipped on.

It's made of six layers of thin, almost sheer material. Each layer is completely see-through when separated, but together, they are opaque.

"Holy fuck, Anna, who knew pregnant chicks could be that sexy?"

"Shut up," I say and roll my eyes.

"I am serious. That dress is really beautiful, and it looks fantastic on you," Giselle replies, and her eyes are wide as she looks me over.

The dress has a deep v that ends just above my swollen belly, showcasing my cleavage and bringing attention to the fact I'm pregnant without making me feel ridiculously unattractive.

In fact, I feel the opposite. She's right. I feel sexy.

"I really love the color," I confess.

"It looks great," she says again.

I'm not someone who needs a lot of compliments to feel good, and I sure as shit am not conceited. But I appreciate my bestie telling me I look good.

I turn and see myself in the mirror, and I'm floored. I am glowing. It's like what they say about pregnant women looking radiant is actually true.

My skin is golden from all my time swimming in the rooftop pool and the brown color of the dress compliments my tan.

I applied a shimmery moisturizer that makes me feel and smell good. Like vanilla orchids and cocoa butter.

There are tiny glass beads sewn on the neckline and the edges of the cap sleeves, as well as on the bottom of the skirt. The dress falls in flirty little layers around mid-thigh, and I am so glad I can still shave by myself.

When I get bigger, I will probably need help. I bite my lip, wondering if husbands do that for their pregnant wives.

Do they help them shave?

I picture Nico in the shower with me, we've taken them together before. But this time I picture him lathering my thighs and calves with thick shave butter and using my razor to take the hair off and, damn, I feel moisture gather between my legs.

Why does that sound so erotic?

I never had a man shave me. But if Nico says yes, I just might let him.

I continue to gnaw on my lip as I slide on a pair of strappy flat sandals and Giselle helps tie them. I still get a little off balance when I lean too far over.

After we style our hair and apply makeup, we are both ready for our prospective dates. But I kind of wish we were going out together.

As if he heard me, my phone chimes and I look to see a text from Nico. I grin at the word *husband*. He entered his contact info into my phone, and I grin every time I see it.

HUSBAND

Something's come up and I'm going to be late getting you. Angel can drive you to the Den, so we don't have to be late for our reservation. Would you be okay with that?

So thoughtful. And the truth is I want to see him so badly, I don't want to wait either.

ANNA

Sure. Is it okay if Giselle comes with me to the Den? I think she has a date or something with Angel later.

HUSBAND

Of course. I can't wait to see you, Rosebud.

ANNA

Awww, you miss me.

HUSBAND

Wife.

ANNA

I miss you, too.

He doesn't reply, and I bite my lip. We never talk about our feelings. But I care deeply for Nico. I know I shouldn't, but I do.

Angel presses the intercom button and his gruff voice filters through the speaker.

"Are you ladies ready to go?" Angel asks.

I watch Giselle straighten her shoulders, and I raise my eyebrows. She is usually the calm, cool, collected one. But something about Angel makes her nervous.

I only hope this doesn't end badly. I'd hate to have my best friend feel weird about seeing me if she and Angel don't work out.

The ride to the Den is quiet, but I catch Angel looking at Giselle's crossed legs in the short, tight dress she's borrowed.

She is ignoring him, and I turn my head, so the

big man doesn't see me grin. Okay, fine, so I'm kind of laughing at him.

It's absurd, but the sexual tension between them is so thick, I swear I can see it.

"Um, did Nico say if he would be there when we get there?" I ask Angel.

"What? Oh, um, no, he didn't say anything to me," Angel grumbles.

The drive is fast after that and Angel holds the door open for me, careful to step aside, so absolutely no part of me touches him while I slide out of the tall seat.

But I notice he is there with his hand out, reaching for Giselle before she can get out after me.

Very interesting.

We are parked in an alley behind the club, but it's paved, and the street is clear of trash and debris. Another hulking security guard stands at a door, holding it open for us.

"After you," Angel says, and I walk first, Giselle following me.

I remember that hallway as the one I walked in that night I first came to settle my brother's debts and my heart squeezes.

So much has happened since then.

Sammy is gone.

I don't have to worry about the bakery anymore.

I'm pregnant.

I'm married.

Hell, I hardly recognize my life anymore. And suddenly, it's not such a bad thing.

I mean, I wasn't exactly living life to the fullest before I got involved with Nico. To be honest, I was barely making ends meet.

The bakery is an obligation. Not something I enjoy. And the bakers have been making it difficult to try to do my job there with their constant threats and demands. Ever since Javi came on board things have been worse.

Sure, Nico and I didn't meet conventionally. But we are together now.

And it just might be the best thing that ever happened to me.

CHAPTER TWENTY-NICO

This fucking bitch won't shut up and I am so over this meeting. Goddamn housing inspector thinks he can shake me down for more money.

He doesn't know I know about his little addiction to a certain escort service. Or the fact he likes to do unsavory things with the women he rents for the evening.

I'm not one to tell anyone how to get off or how to make a little dough. Which is why I paid one of those women quite a hefty fee to film this sick fuck while he was getting his cookies.

Personally, I'm not into golden showers or what-ever the fuck you call it. But if this guy needs a woman to pee on him to get off, that's his business.

However, I can make it his wife's business. In fact, I tell him just that in so many words before I walk out of his office.

"Wait, Nico—"

"Mr. Fury," I snap, my back to him as I straighten my suit jacket.

I know. It's weird, me in a suit, but the truth is I conduct all my legitimate business meetings in suits. I can't just knock around in black t-shirts and jeans and expect people to take me seriously.

So, tailored suits with pristine white shirts and light Italian linen make up much of my summer wardrobe. I usually change before going home, though, and I wonder how Anna will like me in this getup.

"Mr. Fury, please, that video, you won't really tell my wife?"

"Mr. Hamilton, I'm sure I don't know what you mean. Now, I expect the approval stamp to be on those projects we mentioned by noon tomorrow. Give my best to Vivian," I say, naming his wife of thirteen years.

All the shit I know. Fuck. I exhale and walk to my car.

But it weighs on me. All the nasty information I have on the people in power in this fucking city is enough to send the whole infrastructure crumbling down. It would bury them all.

It never fails to amuse me that the more legitimate deals Viper Enterprises takes on, the more aware I become that the business world is infinitely more fucked up than the criminal world.

At least there you know who's who. One bad guy recognizes another in a dark alley, but when you're in a boardroom or a fancy office in city hall, it becomes more difficult to tell.

"Boss?" Tommy asks, holding my door open.

I take it from him and vault into the car. It's eight o'clock, but it's July, so the sun is still out. My fingers are itching, and I recognize the feeling.

It happens every time I'm away from her for too long. I need my Anna. She's my light in all this darkness. She's my good in this world.

With her, it doesn't feel so lonely. So hopeless. So rotten and dirty.

"Drive to the Den," I tell Tommy, looking at the tracking app on my phone to confirm what I already know since Angel already texted me.

Anna is inside the Vipers' base of operations, and I know she's safe there, but I can't help but twitch at the thought of having her in that place.

I need to get over it, though. Because Anna is

mine as much as my crown is. I need to reconcile both sides of my life, and the sooner the better.

Besides, I have yet to introduce my entire crew to my wife, and they need to know. The whole world needs to know who and what she is.

Mine.

Anna is mine. That means she is protected. She is off fucking limits. Untouchable.

Except for me. I'm the only one who gets to touch her, and my blood sings at the truth of those words.

Tommy drives into the alley behind the club, and I open the door before he comes to a stop, leaping out.

I don't even try to hide how eager I am.

I need my wife. *Now.*

I can sense her presence before I see her, and I can't help the intensity on my face as I close the distance between us.

Anna is sitting at my private booth just off the side of the bar. Her face is animated as she talks to an attractive woman with black curls and pale green eyes. It's her friend, Giselle, the one who tossed beer in Angel's face, catching my cousin's attention.

Of course, I already researched her. Hell, I ran background checks on everyone in my wife's life, including those bakers which I owed her an update on.

But all those things I have to tell her leave my brain when I take in her appearance. I'm aware she's pregnant.

Of course, I fucking am.

And I know society likely frowns upon the kind of thoughts going through my head about all the filthy things I want to do to her.

But Anna looks so goddamn fuckable in that flirty little dress she's wearing, I can't help myself.

I catch a glimpse, a flash really, of exposed thigh beneath the table, and my blood heats.

She probably shouldn't be here. Not in this place. She's too good for it. Too good for me.

But I can't help it. I like seeing her there. In my chair. On my throne.

I'm the fucking king of the Vipers, and she's my undisputed queen.

Maria slides a drink over to her, and she nods at something my pretty wife says. I'm glad they're getting along.

I was worried the bartender might be a little salty with my wife after she failed to catch my attention. If Maria is disrespectful in any way to Anna, then I'm going to have to fire her.

But it doesn't look like I have to worry about that, and I'm glad. Good employees are hard to come by.

The Vipers' Den has an average sized staff, but the main bar is important. I need people there I trust. And Maria is a good, honest employee.

"Nico," Anna says my name just as I reach her.

Pleasure shoots through my veins and I grip the back of her neck, dropping my head and kissing her with total and complete ownership.

I feel everyone's eyes on us, and I increase the pressure, earning a moan from my sweet wife's lips. I bring my other hand up, wrapping it around her throat as I lay claim to her mouth.

It's a total dick move, but what can I say?

It's good to be the king.

CHAPTER TWENTY-ONE-ANNA

The Vipers' Den is jam-packed for a Thursday night.

I thought we were just going to split off here, I would meet up with Nico and leave Giselle and Angel to whatever date they have planned.

Instead, Nico isn't here yet, so I slide into the reserved booth Angel points out after we arrive. It's plush black leather and super comfortable.

"Should we be sitting here?" I ask Angel, trying to be heard without shouting over the pounding music, when I notice more than a few eyes darting to us.

"This is the king's table. You belong to the king," he says, as if that clears anything up.

I shoot Giselle a look she knows means *holy shit* because, well, *holy fucking shit.*

This is incredible.

I mean, his statement is definitely chauvinistic. And it shouldn't make me feel anything other than repulsion.

But I do. I feel something else.

I feel pride.

I want to belong to Nico. I don't know if that makes me weak or anti-feminist or what. I just know I have some serious feelings for my husband.

"Hey, what can I get you?" a voice asks, and I turn to see a pretty bartender with straight brown hair and almond shaped eyes staring at me.

I recognize her from the other times I was in the bar before. She seemed hostile then, but some of her edge is gone.

She looks like a puppy who's been corrected.

Then I scold myself for the unkind thought, and I offer a smile.

"Hi, I'm Anna," I say. "This is Giselle, but I call her Sisi."

"What's up?" Giselle nods at her.

"Oh, um, I'm Maria. Can I get you two something to drink?"

"Yes, thank you, I'm parched. Can I have, well, do you have any juice?" I ask.

"Sure. Fresh squeezed orange juice work?" Maria

points out a large citrus juicing machine behind the bar and I grin.

"Oh my God! Yes, please," I reply.

"Since you're doing orange juice, anyway, can I have an Orange Crush?" Giselle asks.

"You bitch," I tease. That is my favorite drink.

"I can make that as a virgin for you," Maria offers, and I nod.

"Yes, yes, please and thank you," I say, wiggling in my seat.

I can't help it. I wiggle when I'm excited.

"You got it," Maria replies, and winks.

Angel is watching us, but he's standing a few feet away. I see a few guys walk up to him. Whatever they are saying, I don't know, but when Angel answers them, each one turns towards us and gives a slight nod of their heads.

Almost like a bow.

I inhale and my body gives a head to toe shiver, but I'm not cold. This is all just so surreal.

A few minutes pass and I'm drinking the sweet, delicious concoction Maria made me.

Giselle moans over how good her drink is, and Maria stays to chat for a while too, before going to help more customers.

She's not the only bartender working tonight, but

she is good and a lot of customers, male customers especially, seem to vie for her attention.

I notice Luc when he comes in. He dips his chin to say hello and I wave, making him and Angel both smile.

"You're such a dork." Giselle snorts, and I roll my eyes.

Whatever.

I'm a friendly girl, I can't help it. The whole nodding thing is for guys. So, waving it is.

Usually, that's the kind of thing I'd agonize over. Feeling like I look foolish or something, but I don't mind at all. I feel content.

Happy even.

Truth is, I missed this. Just hanging out and being with people. Sure, I worked in the office a lot in the bakery, but I used to at least talk to people every day.

I've been lonely stuck in the condo while Nico works, and this is just what I needed. But I realize I need more.

I need my husband.

Tingles dance up my spine and I turn my head as the man himself walks in.

No, walk isn't the right word to describe his progression across the bar. Nico doesn't just move, he moves with purpose.

Like he's prowling. Or maybe even stalking me across the room.

And, oh my, but he is something to behold. My entire body feels lit up and attuned to his every movement.

He is so good looking. More so than any man I have ever seen. His height and his muscular frame make him one of the biggest guys here. Then there's his short haircut, the trimmed beard that only serves to highlight his chiseled features, his hot as fuck tattoos, and his bright blue eyes.

Nico Fury is positively delicious. I want to lick him from head to toe. Every brain cell I have seems to short circuit, as I imagine doing exactly that.

Unwanted doubt starts to creep into my mind. What is he doing with me? This guy can have anyone he wants. I can't believe he really chose me.

I feel special. Honored.

I lick my lips, watching his progression. Aware that all eyes are on him.

The king.

Everyone must know him. Or, if they don't *know him* know him, then they can feel him.

His power. The air of authority that clings to his skin.

They don't seem to question it. They simply move.

It's the right thing to do. I don't see any other course of action.

The crowd just parts for him like the Red Sea. Men and women move out of his way immediately. As for Nico, well, he doesn't slow his speed or alter his course.

He heads straight for me. Each step is deliberate. Every move is predetermined. His expression is intense as he moves, coiling through the throng. And me, well, I'm frozen.

I am completely caught in his thrall, My heart thunders, my pulse races, and my entire body lights up like a fireworks display.

He's close now. Inches away. Then he's right there, and I whisper his name.

"Nico," I say reverently, almost like a prayer.

And maybe I am praying. God help me, Nico Fury is the answer to every single one of mine.

He cups my neck, claiming me publicly with his lips, and I melt into him.

It doesn't matter where we are, I will always cling to this man, to my husband, because, like Angel said earlier, Nico is the king and I belong to him.

CHAPTER TWENTY-TWO-NICO

"Uh, you gonna introduce me?"

I swallow my wife's gasp, and I smile, releasing her lips with one hard, plucking kiss.

"Sorry," she whispers, and her cheeks turn a dusky shade of rose. "Um, Nico, this is Sisi, er, Giselle, my best friend."

She gestures to the woman beside her, and I nod.

"Nice to meet you," I say, shaking her hand briefly.

"Thanks. For everything you're doing for Anna. She's important to me," Giselle says.

"She's important to me, too," I tell her honestly and my eyes go to Anna's.

"You comfortable? Everything okay?" I ask.

"Of course. We had a good day and, uh, Angel drove us right here."

"That's good. You look beautiful," I murmur.

I take the fabric of her sleeve between my fingers and rub the material. It's pretty and soft, just like her.

Anna smiles at me. It's so bright and sincere, it takes my breath away.

"You wanna go to dinner with me?" I ask.

I rub the back of my neck and glance around to see who's listening. But no one is. Angel is talking with Giselle, and Luc is at the bar.

Still, I feel foolish because she's my wife and I shouldn't be nervous about asking her on a date.

But I am.

There's a commotion to my left. Something crashes, the sound of glass breaking reaches my ears. I spin around, careful to make sure I'm blocking Anna.

Angel is already on his feet and striding towards where Luc, my pacifist fucking Council, is beating the shit out of some guy. I see Maria shaking like a leaf. Her back is pressed against the back of the bar as she watches, wide-eyed.

"What's happening?" Anna asks, her tiny hands clutching the back of my coat.

"Nothing. Come on," I say gruffly, standing to my full height while I help her and Giselle out of the booth and direct them towards my office.

I signal to a group of my men, sending some to Angel and Luc, and the rest with me.

They know how to do their jobs.

The crowd is pushed back and I'm able to get my wife and her friend away without incident. I stop at the door before mine and open it.

"Giselle, you can wait here for Angel. This is his office. Don't leave till he comes for you," I tell her.

"Nico," Anna says, and I turn to her.

She looks pale and her hand is on her stomach.

"Are you okay? The baby?"

"Fine. Both fine," she says and reaches for my hand.

I hold hers tight and pull her up the stairs and out to my SUV. Once we're inside the vehicle, I gather her to me and buckle her in.

I'm worried Anna might be scared. And I'm just so fucking mad at myself for having her come to the club in the first place.

Fights don't happen very often. But they aren't unheard of.

Shit.

I hear her yawn and I look down. I blink. She doesn't seem upset.

"Are you tired? Do you wanna skip dinner?"

"Um, no. Well, I mean, yes, I'm pregnant, so I'm always tired," she jokes. "But I am also kind of hungry. Is it okay if we still get food?"

I must look as confused as I am because here, I thought she'd be demanding I take her home, but she's not. Anna bites her lower lip, something she does all the time, and she's so cute when she does it.

But I don't like the idea she might hurt herself, so I tug it free with my thumb.

"You still want to go out to eat?" I ask, because I'm not sure I understand.

"Oh God, I'm sorry. I know I should be upset or something, and maybe you have to go back to check on your guy, but I'm guessing Luc can handle himself, and really, I want to go out with you," she whispers like it's some secret hope or desire she has.

Pride fills me. And something else. I think it's happiness.

"You're so fucking perfect, Rosebud," I say and capture her lips with mine.

I hold her in place with my fingers on her chin and neck, and I content myself with simply kissing her. Even though I am dying to do filthy things to her.

Anna is so damn good, I can't help it. I want to make her dirty.

I want to tear the clothes from her swollen body. Lick her from head to toe. Make her scream my name until she's mindless with need. I want to watch my cum dripping from every orifice.

I want all those things more than I want my next breath. But then, her stomach growls and I know I have to feed her first.

"Take us to *Il Tavolo*," I tell Tommy.

"You got it, Boss."

"Mm. Is that Italian?" she asks.

"Yeah. I thought maybe you'd like some pasta."

"I'd love it," she says, smiling.

I smile back. It doesn't feel as strange anymore. Seems my little wife is a sorceress. She conjures smiles from my lips more easily with every passing day.

I lift our joined hands and kiss her knuckles and love blooms inside my heart at the expression in her eyes.

I have to tell her. And soon.

Dinner was sublime.

We started with tri-color salad and fried calamari. Then, we both had the lobster raviolo in a light cream sauce, followed by a rack of lamb and steamed broccolini.

Everything was delicious. Dessert, though. That was the best.

Nico spoon fed me blood-orange sorbet and I could have cried at how romantic it all was. He moved our chairs close, so close I felt his body pressed into my side.

The suit he wore fit him like a second skin expertly tailored to his muscular frame. I love the way his white silk shirt contrasted with his tattoos.

The thick multi-colored ink is so damn sexy, I can't get enough of it. *Of him.*

I thought I might fall asleep in the car on the way home, but I don't.

I'm sitting up in bed, wearing a tiny slip of a nightgown. It's a shimmery nude material that really leaves nothing to the imagination.

Maybe that's why I am wearing it and nothing else.

I leave off my panties and squirm on top of the bed, biting my lip as I wait for my husband.

I have the blankets turned down, and even though the AC is on full blast I feel overheated.

Nico said he was going to get a glass of water, but it's been a few minutes. I wonder if he got side-tracked by something.

Maybe the bar fight with Luc?

I frown, about to get up when the door to our bedroom opens and Nico strolls in.

Holy. Fuck.

I am really glad I'm still sitting for this.

Nico's eyes are glued to mine. The bright blue is electric and blazing with need. And I tremble.

That look is for me.

His need.

His desire.

That hungry look in his eyes.

It's all for me.

I feel my body respond.

Moisture pools between my legs, my nipples pebble as my breasts swell, and an aching sort of pang twists inside me.

Nico comes to stand at the foot of the bed. He is wearing nothing at all. And I am captivated.

My gaze rakes over him from head to foot. My husband is a gorgeous specimen of man. He's so, so *big*.

Everywhere. He is just huge. His body is corded in thick ropes of muscle. His tattooed skin is on full display, and I already have so many of the designs memorized.

But I want to know them all. I want to trace them with my fingers and my tongue.

"You look fucking perfect in my bed, Wife."

Heat flares inside me. I love it when he calls me *Wife*.

Like he's proud of me. Proud to call me his.

I want him to be, I realize. I crave it. His approval. His desire. It's better than chocolate.

He has an ice bucket in his big, inked up hands and his lips tilt up in a wicked grin.

"You said you were hot in the car. I came to cool you off, Rosebud."

Excitement rushes through my veins like water through a newly broken dam.

"I do feel really hot," I whisper.

Holy. Shit.

Nico looks like some kind of ancient warrior, or a demigod. His entire body bristles with energy and muted strength.

I wish I could be strong like him.

He lifts an ice cube in one hand, taking my foot off the bed with the other. His stunning blue eyes find mine, and he slides the cold little block up my leg, starting at my ankle.

I gasp at the chill tingling along my skin.

Then I moan at the heat filling me because of it.

He hums deep in his chest. It's a sound I like. One of approval.

Nico sets the bucket down. But I can see another ice cube in his hand. He takes that one, kneeling between my legs, and he rubs it up my other leg.

"So hot. Aren't you, Little Mama?"

"Yes, Nico," I whimper.

He's teasing my inner thighs with cold fingertips, and I wonder if both ice cubes are already melted.

"Are you hot here?" he asks, and he coasts his icy fingers over my pussy.

"Oh God," I moan, lifting my hips, but he pulls back.

"Not God, Rosebud. Who am I?"

"Nico. You're my Nico."

"That's right. I'm yours."

He reaches down and comes up with another ice cube. This time, he puts it in his mouth, his eyes twinkling with mischief.

I want to beg him to touch me. But I don't have to.

He's already bending down, his gigantic hands wrap around my thighs, pressing me open, then I feel it. The ice cube in his mouth. He slides it up and down my slit with his tongue, teasing my clit, dragging it down to my asshole.

Then he growls.

Like a beast. Nico is between my thighs, and he literally rumbles with his mouth on my pussy.

And it's like, it's so good.

I'm so close to coming. His fingers spear my sex. And I feel something else. His pinky maybe? And it's teasing my puckered hole.

I never had anyone inside my ass before. But suddenly, I'm curious.

I want Nico there.

As if he can read my mind, I feel something small and cold. It's pressing against me there.

Then it's inside and I yell his name. It's too much. It's not enough.

It's sensory overload.

My hands are searching for purchase in his short hair, but I can't find any, so I just grab his ears while he sucks on my clit.

His pinky is inside me now, pushing in where the ice cube lubed the way. And it feels strange, but good.

His other fingers are working inside of me, and one orgasm turns into two.

CHAPTER TWENTY-FOUR-NICO

S weet God in heaven my wife is so fucking hot for me.

I need to possess this woman in every way, and fucking her virgin ass with my pinky while I feast on her dripping slit is just the thing to satisfy the beast in me. The thing that won't be happy until I claim every inch of her.

Anna moans and bucks against me. Her fingers grip my ears and fuck, that hurts, but I kind of like it.

Her juices drip down my chin, and it turns me on so much, I feel precum leaking all over the sheet.

But I don't want to spend myself on the mattress like some fucking green punk.

I pull my hands free of her and slide up her body.

Cock in hand, I notch myself inside her tight entrance.

"You ready for me? Tell me."

I need her to say it, even though I know the answer. Hell. I can feel it dripping all over my dick.

"Yes. I'm ready. I need you, Nico. Please."

Fuck.

I love it when she says that. I slam my hips forward, driving my cock all the way inside her.

I'm not gentle tonight. I can't be.

I grip her hips, tilting them up. I don't want to crush her, but I have to fuck her. Making love is not an option when I'm this amped.

So, I rut into her like the monster I am.

Anna accepts it. She takes me in. Her tiny hands clutch at my sides, and I stroke into her deeper, rougher, harder with every move.

"Nico."

She pants my name.

"Nico."

This time, she whines.

"Say it again, Anna. Scream it," I grind against her. And she does.

She fucking screams it as she comes, and her cunt clenches around me like a goddamn vise.

I moan as I follow her into carnal bliss. I can't

stop rocking my hips, though. It's like my dick is determined to wring out every drop of pleasure it can from our bodies.

I grind into her, the sound of our slick flesh sliding together fills my ears. That and the hammering of my heart inside my chest.

I have my arms around her now, and I'm holding her close as I dare, careful of the baby. My face is buried between her neck and her shoulder, and I close my teeth around her flowery vanilla cocoa butter scented skin.

"Ouch! You bit me," she says, but I can hear her smile.

My balls give one final squeeze, and I rock into her sensitive clit once more. Anna moans.

Finally, after several long minutes, I lift my head.

Her face is flushed, but her eyes are sparkling. She hums and licks her lip and I can't stop myself from kissing her.

The way she opens up for me, like a flower in the sunlight, fucking humbles me. I feel it all the way to my core, and I am so Goddamn grateful for it. For her.

I don't know what I did to deserve her, I'm sure I don't. But I know she's mine. This woman was made for me.

Every other thought I have about us not belonging together or me bringing her down, well, I shove all that shit right out of my head.

There is no other option for us now. Anna is mine and I'm hers.

I lean back, sliding my spent cock from her slippery heat, and I rise to my knees.

"Hold on," I tell her before she can try to move.

I slide my fingers up her thighs, tracing the stream of our mixed cum and pressing it into her slit.

"So fucking sexy." I groan.

Anna squirms, but her breath catches, and I know she's turned on.

"Should I tell you how you look with our combined cum leaking out of your puffy pink cunt, Rosebud?" I murmur, and her eyes glaze over.

She licks her lips, and I spread the thick, sticky mess around, coating my fingers and pressing them back inside her.

I graze her clit, and she bucks her hips.

"You're such a dirty girl, aren't you?" I growl, working my fingers in and out of her clenching sex.

Fuck.

I reach up with my other hand and tug on the

straps of her nightgown. They snap, freeing her glorious tits.

They've grown with her pregnancy. Her areolas have darkened, and her nipples are larger.

They bounce around while I fuck her on my hand.

Goddamn.

She looks so fucking hot. I lean forward and lift one of her heavy tits, sucking it into my mouth. She tastes so sweet.

She's everywhere. My head is filled with her.

"I want to shove my dick between these tits. Come all over your face. Will you let me do that, Rosebud? Will you let me fuck these titties," I snarl, as visions of doing that swim in my head.

She moans. Anna's eyes widen. And I swear she nods.

Christ.

I should be spent after the fucking we just shared. But my dick is hard again, and I let her tit slide from my mouth with a popping sound.

Yes. I need to fuck her tits. I need to claim her everywhere.

"Nico, please," she moans, and she's rocking her hips in time with my hand.

"That's it. Show me how good this feels. Come for me, Wife."

She does and I move. I pull Anna into a kneeling position on all fours. Just like the first time we had sex, only she's facing me.

I've fondled her sweet breasts before. Squeezed and teased her mounds, tugged her nipples. And I know she likes it. I know they are extra sensitive now, too.

But I haven't done this to her.

And I need to.

I slam my mouth to hers, feel her quiver against me. Then I slide underneath her, so her cunt and ass are positioned just below my face and her heavy tits are dragging across my thighs.

She moves where I place her. Bending to my will, knowing where I need her, and needing it just as much. At least I fucking hope so.

I wish I could straddle her and do this, but I won't. Not while she's pregnant.

But after she has the baby. Then I'll revisit that little plan.

Once I feel her breasts surround my cock, I start to thrust. Her tits are so soft. They feel exquisite hugging the velvet skin of my cock.

"That's it, Rosebud. Squeeze those tits together.

Let me feel them surrounding me," I grunt and slide my dick between them.

While that's happening, I swipe my hand through her slippery folds, lubing my fingers as I lick and tease her pretty pink asshole.

Anna moans, her mouth closes over my head as my cock slides up and down between her tits. She keeps doing that, dropping open mouthed kisses on my tip while I fuck her tits.

Jesus H. Christ.

I'm gonna come. I'm gonna come soon. It feels too good not to let go.

This is by far the hottest thing I have ever done with a woman.

So, with one finger in her ass, two in her slit, and my dick between her tits while she laps at my slitted head, I lose control for the first time in my life.

Ropes of hot white cum shoot from my cock. My release coats her neck, her tits, her belly.

And what does my wife do? How does she react to this primordial display?

Well, her hot little cunt clamps down on my fingers, and then Anna comes, too.

She comes hard.

So fucking perfect.

My Rosebud. My Anna.
So fucking mine.

The days melt into one another as the weekend passes. Nico's been home the whole time, but I know this little slice of heaven will soon pass.

He's far too busy to play hooky for very long. And I get that. But I don't want to go back to being bored.

"What's going on?" he asks, looking up from the banana-blueberry-cinnamon pancake batter he's working on.

I woke up with a craving, and my awesome husband loves to feed me. It's a win-win, really.

"I was just thinking, you know, I've never not worked."

"You mean at the bakery?"

"I mean, in general. I always had something going

on, school, projects, clubs, the bakery. Anyway, it's weird for me, not working."

"Um, Rosebud, I hate to point out the obvious, but you're growing a tiny human inside of you. I'd say that's plenty of work," he counters.

I grin and roll my eyes, waving my hand and my brand new wedding ring catches my eye. It's so damn pretty. And it's perfect. As if he knew I would be concerned over a stone scratching the baby, he managed to find me a ring where the gems are embedded in the platinum band.

And he didn't get me diamonds. No, he got me a solitary sapphire, as blue and crystalline as his eyes. It's so Nico. And like him, it's perfect. Set so deep in the band, it doesn't catch on anything.

I fucking love it.

This man.

"Yeah," I continue, "but what about after?"

"After what? Oh, after he's born?" Nico asks, scooping the first spoonful of batter onto the hot griddle.

"Yeah. what do I do after he's born?"

"Besides raising our baby together, you mean? And I am not saying that to be a sexist jerk—"

"I know that," I interrupt him.

Nico is a lot of things, but I know he isn't one of

those men who thinks their women should be in the kitchen or doing laundry. I can tell just by the fact he's always cooking.

"Okay, good. Well, I don't know then. What do you want to do? Is there something in particular?"

"Well, I know there is the bakery," I hedge.

"Did you want to go back to work at the bakery? The woman Angel found to run it is doing great. Especially now that we canned that fucker, Javi."

"Yeah, I talked to her a few times. She is great. And no, I admit, I don't want to go back to work at the bakery."

"Okay," he says, handing me a plate with a short stack of perfectly golden pancakes.

"Thank you."

My stomach growls and I grin as I douse them in butter and syrup.

"My pleasure, Rosebud. But finish telling me what you mean."

"Okay, so, actually I kind of want to, well, it's stupid," I start, taking a sip of juice.

"Anna. Nothing you say is stupid. Now, just tell me. What do you want to do?"

"It's just, I, uh, I like to sew," I say, and I can see his surprise.

"You can sew?"

"Yeah, my grandma taught me."

"The quilt on the bed, did you make that? And the pillowcases?" he asks, and I see him piecing it together.

"Yeah," I tell him shyly.

"Holy shit, Anna. That's fucking awesome. You're an artist."

"I wouldn't say that."

"I would. Everything you make is beautiful. Why didn't you tell me before?"

"I wasn't trying to keep it from you, it just never came up," I tell him the truth.

Usually, when Nico and I are in the same room, it's all I can do to remember my own name. The man makes my brain fuzzy.

"Alright, well, we can set up a whole sewing workroom for you right here. We have the space," he says nonchalantly.

Like this isn't some life altering big deal.

I learned to sew as a kid, but my father never took it seriously. I don't think Sammy ever mentioned it at all unless he needed me to hem something.

Excitement hums in my brain, and I think of all the pretty things I've been wanting to try out for the baby's room. Which is something else we need to talk about.

"We do? Um, what about a nursery?" I ask.

"I thought the bedroom next to ours would work. What do you think?" he asks.

And when he sits beside me, I tell him what I think. And he listens.

For the first time in my life, someone listens to what I have to say and I feel important. I feel cherished. Like I matter.

Nico doesn't dismiss me or my opinions. He encourages them. He asks questions about what I need and what I like.

"You would really do all this for me?"

"Yeah, of course I would, Rosebud."

"Why?" I have to know.

He's floored me with all this. I am so full of emotions, I'm near to bursting. My heart is right there on my sleeve, and I can hardly see him for the tears filling my eyes.

"Because, Anna, you're my wife. You're the mother of my child."

Nico stands up, taking our empty plates and loading them into the sink. Then he turns back to look at me, his blue eyes blazing.

"But most of all, it's because I love you, Anna Fury."

Nico disappears as tears fill my eyes, I drop my gaze hiccupping as I openly sob like a complete idiot.

But he's there suddenly, his strong arms around me, grounding me, supporting me.

He tips my head back, wiping my tears.

"I love you."

He says it again and I can't hold it in anymore.

"I love you, too," I reply, and I throw myself at him.

Thank fuck the king of Vipers is fast as he is strong. I smile through my tears as Nico kisses me sweetly, murmuring his love for me the whole while.

His big hands cup my belly and I place mine on top of his, laughing as our baby kicks to greet his papa.

"I love you both," he says, dropping to his knees, and Nico kisses my stomach.

And I swoon on my feet.

"Easy, Little Mama."

He steadies me. His smile is wide, and I bask in it.

So, this is what happy feels like.

CHAPTER TWENTY-SIX-NICO

"**I** don't give a fuck what Sanchez says. He did what he did. Now, he can fuck off," I growl.

She loves me.

"Boss, he wants a meeting."

"No meeting," I say.

Anna loves me.

I rap my knuckles against the desk and expel a breath.

I can't just fucking sigh like a high school kid.

But this fucking meeting has gone on too long. It's just Angel and Luc, business as usual, a daily recount of events and things that needed tending to.

But I want to leave.

My wife said she's in love with me.

And I want to crow at the top of my lungs. I want

to beat my chest with my fists. Strut around like a goddamn rooster.

"Uh, Boss, there is something else," Luc hesitates.

"What?"

"Maria. She's been hiding something," he says.

"And?"

I know the little bartender has been hiding something. It's probably why she set her cap at me at first.

"I don't know, Nico. But that scuffle the other day? The guy I fucked up is a scout for Sanchez," Luc says.

"So, you think Maria is working for Sanchez?"

I frown, and Luc glares at me before remembering his place. He averts his gaze.

"I don't know," he says honestly.

"We had Maria vetted like everyone else," Angel adds, but I can see he's brooding.

He has other things on his mind. A curly haired, green-eyed thing in particular, I'd wager.

Anna hasn't mentioned Giselle to me recently, so I don't know what's up with them. But Angel's been quiet, and a quiet Angel is usually not a good thing.

"Okay, we done?" I ask, eager to leave.

"Not hardly," Luc says, and continues to run through the projected numbers on several projects Viper Enterprises is involved in.

"That's all fine, Luc. Send me a fucking email next time."

"Back to our other business, Boss. There's been rumors," Angel says.

"What rumors?"

"Callahan's boys are expecting a big shipment, but they're not keen on giving us our twenty percent for safe passage at the docks."

"They're not, huh?"

"Nope. Sanchez offered protection for only ten percent. Says he's the new man in town," Angel adds, and red seeps into my vision.

Fuck that little upstart motherfucker.

First, my warehouse. Next, he insults me? I roll my neck. This is all bullshit. But I can't let it slide.

"Shut it down," I snarl.

"The dock?"

Angel's eyebrows go sky high when I give the order. Shutting the dock is dangerous for everyone. But if these assholes want to play. I'll play. And I'll fucking win.

I nod and stand.

I'm done here. I need my wife.

"Can you believe it? Less than two months and he'll be here."

"You're so amazing," Nico says, lifting our joined hands to his lips and kissing my knuckles.

The doctor gives us a smile, then leaves the room so I can get dressed. Nico helps.

The second he realized I'd have to be naked for my appointments, he started coming to every single one.

He already chose this doctor, and I'm glad. She has an excellent bedside manner, but it didn't escape my notice everyone in her office is female.

My sexy husband is as possessive about me as I feel about him, and it makes me love him even more.

"You good?" he asks.

Nico helps me stand once my panties are on and my swing dress is back in place. I slide my feet into my sandals, and I nod.

"Yeah, I feel great."

And I do.

The baby is healthy, and my belly is starting to round out like other pregnant women.

We go home. Nico makes me breakfast for dinner. Scrambled eggs, sausage, and pancakes, these are made with strawberries and chocolate chips.

We eat at the counter. And we talk.

I love that I'm learning so much about him. That he's so open to sharing with me. I want to know everything.

"So, I know you're the, um, king of the Vipers," I mumble, a little embarrassed to be saying this out loud. "But what does that mean?"

"What do you think it means?" he counters.

"I don't know. I assume you do illegal stuff?" I squeak the question.

"You're not wrong. But I've learned that illegal, or legal, is only a matter of time. Laws change. And sometimes people wearing collars and badges are the worst crooks," he says, and I nod.

I agree.

"Do you, uh, do you hurt people?" I ask.

"Sometimes."

He doesn't shy away. He is very still, his eyes on mine, but he answers. And I love him for it.

"Do you use a gun?"

"Sometimes. But I prefer fists or a blade."

"Why?"

"It's personal that way. And killing should always be personal," he says nonchalantly.

"So, you kill people?"

"If I have to."

I wait a beat, absorbing the fact my husband just admitted to being a murderer.

It doesn't bother me. But it should. I feel like maybe I understand Nico enough to know he wouldn't kill someone without a reason.

"I'll never lie to you about who I am, Rosebud. But I won't tell you all of it. It could put you in danger, do you understand?"

"Yeah. I understand."

I think about what he's already admitted to me about Sammy. About wanting me and that being the reason he took his marker.

I should be angry. But I'm not.

If it wasn't Nico, it would have been someone else. The assholes who killed him probably, and I actually feel sort of grateful to my brother for bringing me and Nico together.

I probably need all kinds of therapy for that. But not now.

"Have you, um, found who is responsible for Sammy?" I murmur.

"No one is claiming it. But we're working on it. I promise you," he says, and squeezes my hand.

"That reminds me. There is some stuff going on right now with a rival of mine, Sanchez. He wants my territory, but he won't get it."

"Are you okay?" I ask.

Fear flashes through me. And worry. For him. I can't imagine a world without my husband, and I don't want to.

"Of course, I'm fine. But while this is going on, I need to know where you are at all times. No leaving the condo without telling me. And absolutely no going anywhere without a bodyguard."

"Okay."

"I'm serious. I need you safe, Wife. Understand?"

"Yeah. I understand."

"Anything else you want to ask me?" He smiles and my heart thuds in my chest.

"Did you marry me just to give the baby a name?

I mean, I know you love me now, but you couldn't have loved me then."

I make a noise I intended as a laugh, but it's something between sob and whimper.

"It was one of the reasons," he says, and he moves closer.

"What's the other?"

I ask as he cups my cheeks in his hands.

"Don't you know?"

I shake my head.

"Because, Rosebud, you were mine from the first moment I saw you. You're all I need, all I want. I love you, Wife. You're my everything."

"I love you, too," I say and sigh into his kiss.

Nico envelops me in his embrace and I feel him sink into every part of me.

My heart. My body. My mind, My soul.

I am so in love with this man. He ends the kiss with a moan and presses his forehead to mine.

"I'll finish cleaning up. Go put on something comfortable, and we'll watch TV."

I change into a soft maternity pajama short set and snuggle next to Nico on the enormous sofa to watch an old movie with Katherine Hepburn and Cary Grant.

It's a romcom with a wonderful supporting cast of characters and there's even a dinosaur and a leopard.

It's hilarious. I'm surprised Nico likes it, but really, I shouldn't be.

My husband has a lot more depth than I think he gives himself credit for.

The sun is setting outside, and I doze off before the film is over. I stir when I feel Nico lift me, but he brushes his lips over my temple and tells me to go back to sleep as he carries me to bed.

It seems ludicrous that I'm so at ease with an admitted murderer. And yeah, it's entirely possible Nico is a little crazy.

But I'm surprisingly okay with that.

I love him.

I love everything about him.

His unhinged tendencies.

His dark parts.

All the good and the bad.

And I hear my husband whisper the last part of our vows against my temple as he kisses me and tucks me in, and I fall into a deeper, more contented sleep than I ever have with our baby growing right under my heart.

"Till death do us part, Rosebud."

And my soul rejoices at his vow.

It feels so right. It's what I always wanted, and he is just what I need.

CHAPTER TWENTY-EIGHT-NICO

"How long will you be gone for?" Anna asks, her eyes bright with unshed tears as I rush home to explain there's been an emergency.

The doctor just told her she needs to be on bed rest for the final three weeks of her pregnancy and here I am abandoning her, and I feel like a miserable piece of fucking shit.

"I'm sorry. I'm not going far. Just Boston. A business associate has news he will only share in person. There's a whole fucking process, it's all bullshit pomp, but I can't ignore it. Tell me you understand, and you forgive me?"

I fucking beg her.

"Nico, hush," she chides. "There's nothing to

forgive. Go do what you have to then come home to me, safe and sound. Got it? Tell me."

Her whispered demand is so fucking hot, and I nod my head because yeah, I got it.

"I'll always come back to you both," I tell her, and I mean it.

I mean it so fucking much. Anna is cupping my face in her hands. I turn my head to kiss her palm, but she pulls me close, and I let her lips claim mine, and fuck, it feels incredible.

I've never let anyone close to me like this. I drink her in, letting her fill all those deep, empty places inside me.

I'm used to the dark, to being on my own. Even with Angel and Luc and all the Vipers working for us, I never let anyone in.

Just Anna.

My Anna.

She is my home.

She's my heart.

My everything.

"I love you, Nico. Stay safe, Husband," she says, and I kiss her again.

"You have your phone," I say for the second time and she nods.

"Yes, and don't worry, Mrs. Pirillo is staying just

like you asked her to," she tells me, naming our housekeeper.

The woman is in her sixties and has been working for me for a decade now. I have six armed guards in the building. Two outside the door, two on the roof, and two in the lobby.

They've all been vetted. Twice.

These are men I know. Men who have worked for me for years. Men that I trust.

And just because I'm a special brand of fucking psycho where my wife is concerned, I already told them in graphic detail the ways I will end their miserable lives should a single fucking hair on her head be harmed while I'm gone.

"I'll be back soon, Rosebud."

I fucking mean it.

"I'll be counting the minutes."

My heart squeezes. Anna means it, too.

For the first time in my life, I feel connected to someone. Like a chain is tying me to this woman, pulling me back from the abyss, and it feels fucking great.

Christ, I love her.

CHAPTER TWENTY-NINE-ANNA

My face hurts from smiling.

Mrs. Pirillo is helping me set up my brand new sewing machine in the bedroom. This one is lightweight and compact.

It fits perfectly on the rolling side table Nico ordered for me along with a bunch of other thoughtful gifts that just make me love him all the more.

There are spools of brightly colored thread, yards of fabric of all patterns and textures, and books on quilting and sewing crafts.

I already started on the baby's quilt, and I think Nico will like it. I chose soft blues, greens, and ivory for the colors, with the occasional burst of butter yellow.

The design is a simple Maypole pattern. Mrs. Pirillo is helping me, so it's done in time.

I send all this to Nico via text, and he always responds immediately. He *oohs* and *aahs* in all the appropriate places.

Giselle visits me. Maria comes with her, and I learn the two of them have formed a friendship. It seems some things have been happening while I've been confined to the condo.

"Wow, you look, um, swollen," Giselle blurts, and that's it.

I just start crying. Like full on, body wracking sobs.

"Sisi, are you for real?" Maria scolds her and wraps her arms around me.

"No, she's right," I try to say, but my voice is garbled with all my crying.

"Hush. You look great." Maria lies.

"I'm big as a house. This baby is gigantic, and he's going to break my vagina when he comes out. Everything is swollen, and I can't even fit in any of my maternity clothes. And I miss my husband. I just want him back home."

"Hey, it's okay. Anna, you're growing a person. You look fucking gorgeous," Giselle says.

"Yeah, and Nico will be back soon. Luc told me they're almost done," Maria adds.

"Luc told you?"

"Uh, yeah, it's complicated."

"What about you? How's Angel?" I ask Giselle, but my best friend turns her head.

"I don't know how Angel is. Why would I know? He's not my boyfriend and I am nothing to him," she snaps and just like that I am done crying.

"Um, I guess I missed something while I've been here, huh?"

"Yeah, you could say that," Maria confesses.

They stay and we eat steamed veggies and roasted chicken without salt, since I have to avoid it. It's okay, but it makes me want to cry again.

An entire week passes, and I miss Nico even more.

Working on the baby's room helps, but it doesn't make up for him being away. I show him pictures of the little teddy bear I just finished.

The phone rings, and I answer.

"Wife."

His voice is so clear, and I close my eyes, savoring it.

"Nico," I reply.

"Talk to me, Rosebud. I need to hear your sweet voice."

"What's going on over there? Are you almost done?"

I hate that I sound so needy. But I am needy. And I miss him.

"I'm afraid things got a little complicated, but it shouldn't be too long now. We, uh, we found who got to Sammy, Baby."

"You did?" I whisper, and my heart squeezes.

"Yes. It's the same group causing trouble in other areas. Seems like your brother borrowed money from one of their guys, and they aren't the type to take IOUs."

"Poor Sammy," I say, and offer a silent prayer for my brother's soul.

"Yeah. These guys are bad news. You're staying put, right?"

"Yeah. I'm just plugging away. Growing like a weed, too. You won't recognize me when you see me," I mutter.

"I'm sorry I'm missing it. I'll be back soon as I can. Shit. I gotta go."

"Okay, love you—"

But he already hung up, and I frown.

It's not like him to hang up without saying *I love*

you, but I let it go. Maybe someone walked in or something.

I frown as Mrs. Pirillo comes to say goodnight. She shows me the final pieces we need to put together for the baby's quilt, and I smile.

"We can start the curtains tomorrow," I tell her, and she nods.

"Yes, Mrs. Fury."

I've asked her to call me Anna, but she won't, so I just smile and tell her goodnight.

I turn on another classic film, seems I'm addicted, and Nico has such a wonderful collection to choose from. I lay back and sigh, missing my husband, and I think about how big this bed is without him even as I snuggle my body pillow, wrapping it around me to support my back and belly.

"Love you, Husband," I whisper, hoping wherever he is, he can feel my love for him.

The next day, I'm crampy and achy, and when I get up to pee, I almost fall down. There's a red smear in my panties.

That's when I start to panic.

CHAPTER THIRTY-NICO

My cell phone buzzes, but I'm looking across at the boss from one of the oldest Boston crime families, Liam O'Doyle, and I can't afford to fucking blink.

His wrinkled face resembles a fucking Shar-pei, and I immediately clench my jaw, so I don't laugh at the image floating around my brain.

This sonovabitch is behind Sanchez's sudden power grab, and I know it. I just need him to admit it.

Stupid prick has a daughter he's been dangling in my face. Fucker thinks I'm interested, and I'm inclined to let him think whatever he wants. As long as I get what I want and that's info on where Sanchez is hiding out.

The prick vacated his known residences and haunts. My guys have been searching for days.

If O'Doyle is hiding him, I need to know. And if that means lying to the old piece of shit, I can do that with no problem.

Margaret O'Doyle is twenty-two and vapid as fuck. She's years too young for me, or any man, really. Hell, she doesn't know her own mind and all her purring and bedroom eyes mean jack shit to me.

But I sit. And I pretend. I fucking lie because I have responsibilities and obligations. People I need to keep safe.

My wife is sitting home swollen with our baby, and I have to play up to this prick and it is making me furious.

But Angel and Luc just confirmed what I already suspected. Anna's brother. That fucking prick baker. The arson at her old place. My warehouse explosion. All of it leads back to Sanchez. And Sanchez has already proven he will kill people.

"So, you see, Mr. Fury. I can't help you, not unless perhaps a merger can be made," O'Doyle says, gesturing to his daughter.

She's sitting beside him, wearing a bright green spandex dress and looking like she belongs in a St. Patty's Day parade or something.

Inwardly, I cringe. Outwardly, I show no emotion.

But I need to end Sanchez. To eliminate the threat against me and my wife and unborn son. And I need to do it sooner rather than later.

But this old Irish mafia douchebag is protecting him. Suddenly I am not feeling so patient. My phone buzzes again.

I glance down and see twenty messages in the last five minutes. The last one is from the guard I left in charge of Anna's security team.

"Fury, are you hearing me? Maybe this isn't a good time. Maybe your mind is elsewhere," he says, but I am already on my feet.

I ignore him and I reread the text without understanding.

Something happened. Something went wrong. I don't know what, and I can't fucking breathe.

Thunder is roaring in my ears as I race down the hall to find Angel and Luc.

"What?" my cousin says.

I toss the phone at him and jump into the SUV. Angel and Luc get in after me as I order Tommy to drive to the private airport.

My world is crashing down around me. If anything happens to Anna or the baby—no, I can't allow myself to spiral down that motherfucker of a rabbit hole.

It's like fate is laughing at me. I finally have the one thing I wanted, a real home, and I might lose her while wasting my fucking time here.

I am so mad. I am so goddamn mad. But I can't focus on that.

My Anna is in an ambulance. She's probably scared. Probably hurting. And I'm in this shithole of a town talking to some washed up mafia chump while he dicks around with me.

Motherfucker.

"Sever ties with the O'Doyle's," I bark out the order.

"What?" Angel asks.

"I want you to cut them off from every fucking port we own, every connection we have. He's hiding Sanchez, and that makes him my enemy, too. Do it now," I command.

"Yes, Boss," Luc says.

My Council grabs his phone to get things rolling on his end. I see Angel do the same and I should feel some sort of mollification, but I don't.

Fuck this.

I close my eyes and force my boiling rage to a low simmer. My wife needs me and I have to get to the Jersey City Medical Center as fast as possible.

"Tell Gio to get the plane fired up," Angel says into his cell phone.

Good thing he remembers to call ahead.

I can't even think, let alone speak. But ten minutes later we board the plane at the same time Anna arrives in the Emergency Room.

I'm so fucking mad. And I'm afraid. Really afraid.

I haven't felt that kind of fear in a very long time.

What if something happens to Anna or the baby?

What if she blames me?

What if she leaves me?

Panic has me struggling for breath, and I ignore the stares of my men. They don't know. They don't fucking understand.

Anna is my life. I can't lose her. I won't. I fucking refuse.

The plane ride is too long, and I don't bother with the car. From the airport where we land, I take a helicopter right to the hospital.

By the time I arrive, I am sweating through my shirt. I ditched my suit jacket somewhere, I don't fucking know or care.

My sweet Anna is lying in a hospital bed, and she looks pale and weak. Giselle and Maria are both there, and I am grateful to them, but I don't want them there. I want them gone.

I glare at them and stride for my wife.

"Anna," I say, and she opens her eyes.

I expect her usual bright whiskey brown gaze with flecks of gold glittering in the warm depths, but her eyes aren't shining today.

They look dull and lifeless. The whites of her eyes are red from crying.

"Nico," she murmurs like she can't believe I am there and tries to sit up.

"Rosebud," I murmur and wrap her up in my arms, holding her tight to me.

"It's okay, Baby. I'm here. Hush," I say, kissing her head while she cries against my chest.

I know the baby is alright. I read the medical report while I was in the air. It was just some spotting and Braxton-Hicks contractions. They want to keep her overnight to monitor them both.

When I was on my way to the hospital, I called and had her moved into a private room but allowed her friends to visit until I could get there.

But now I am here.

And I want everyone else out.

Angel and Luc know me. They know my nature,

and I'm sure they can see how fucking close I am to losing it. It's happened, albeit infrequently.

But no, I would never be violent towards a woman or women. I just need Anna to myself. I have to make sure she's okay, see it with my own eyes.

I see them take the two women outside. Anna is too distraught to notice, and that's okay.

My job is to calm her down. To be there for her. And I failed. But I won't. not anymore.

She says something, and I can't understand her. The antiseptic smell inside the stark white hospital is dizzying. I hate it. So, I bury my nose in her hair, and I breathe my wife in.

"What is it, Rosebud? I can't hear you when you talk into my shirt."

"I'm sorry. I'm so sorry, Nico, I panicked, and they called you and I didn't mean to make such a big deal about this," she says, and I am stunned.

"What are you talking about, Baby?"

My chest is tight. Is she really apologizing to me?

Of all the reactions I expected from Anna, having her sob into my shirt saying sorry for interrupting my business wasn't even in the top ten.

I hold her closer, kissing her teary cheeks.

"I know you're busy and you were on an important trip, and I shouldn't have let them call you," she says and I can't take it.

"Hey, hey, no. Hush, Rosebud. Hush now. I'm the one who's sorry. You needed me and I wasn't here. I'm so fucking sorry, Baby," I tell her and rock her gently in my arms.

I thought I was going to have to fight to keep her here. That I was going to have to beg and plead, and don't get me wrong, I would have.

I will.

But my beautiful Anna isn't talking about leaving me. She's clinging to me, and I feel about ten feet tall.

This woman. This good, beautiful woman.

I don't know what I did in this life to deserve her. Truth is, I don't.

God knows, I don't.

But I'm not letting her get away from me. Not now, not ever.

"I'm sorry I wasn't here when you got scared. But I will be. From now on, I will be," I tell her, and I mean every word.

My anger at Sanchez and O'Doyle triples as I hold my wife's hand throughout the checkout process. The doctor says we can leave, and I am more than ready. I want her home.

Safe and sound. Where I can protect her.

"Ready?" I ask, and Anna nods.

She looks tired, but content. And always so pretty. To me, she's the most beautiful thing in the world.

I don't wait for the wheelchair, I just scoop her up in my arms. Anna lets out a weak protest.

But she's starting to know me by now, and instead of repeating her objections, she just wraps her arms around my neck and lays her head on my shoulder.

Leaning on *me*.

Trusting *me*.

And it is everything.

CHAPTER THIRTY-ONE-ANNA

"So, how's the second round of bedrest treating you?"

Giselle comes into the bedroom with a tiny stuffed elephant in hand.

"Hey, Sisi," I reply with a tired smile.

"Can I get you two ladies anything before I head out?" Nico asks from the doorway.

"I'm okay," I whisper, and he dips his chin, waiting for Giselle to answer.

"I'm good too."

I'm having a difficult time believing I could be this lucky. Ever since we came home from the hospital, he's been right by my side, or he's had one of my friends come over to sit with me. And our housekeeper, Mrs. Pirillo, has basically moved in.

Either way, I'm never alone. And the doctor has been making house calls.

I feel so pampered. Protected. And it doesn't even matter if it's for the baby or for me, because knowing how much Nico wants our son makes me love him all the more.

His blue eyes sparkle with intensity as he walks over to me and slides his hand around the back of my neck, tipping my face towards him for a kiss.

We haven't fooled around since before my false alarm, and I miss him. I miss the intimacy. But I get it.

The doctor says no heavy physical activity, and sex with Nico is always *heavy* and very, very physical.

Sigh.

"Alright, you ready to rock this Cosmo quiz?" Giselle asks, pulling out one of my favorite magazines.

"They still make those?"

"Hell yeah," she says, and I grin.

We spend the next hour laughing over who our ideal boyfriend is, and it turns out we're both more into fictional men than actual men.

But the editors at Cosmopolitan are wrong.

Nico is a real man, and I am so into him.

CHAPTER THIRTY-TWO-NICO

I listen as Luc and Angel give me their reports on our search for Sanchez.

O'Doyle isn't taking me cutting him off and rejecting his daughter lying down. That asshole has been trying to get others to align against me.

It's slow going for him, but it's only a matter of time before some young punk thinks he can defeat me. So, we hit them. And we hit them hard.

But not how they expect.

I don't send my guys to rough up theirs. I don't burn their warehouses. Or attack their families.

Nope.

I don't need to resort to violence.

I can do that. I am more than capable.

And I am willing.

More than.

Especially when I think of how scared my wife was when I was wasting my fucking time in Boston.

But I don't. Because I'm not looking for a war. I'm simply making a point.

The Vipers aren't the only game in town, but we are the motherfucking strongest.

Life is good when everyone can drink from the only water source in town.

But I control the ports. So, to get my point across, I close the gates. I let everyone feel who has the real power.

Power isn't in how many city employees or government officials I have in my pocket. It isn't in how many guns I have, or able-bodied soldiers.

Money is power. And whoever controls the ports controls the money.

If people can't ship or receive their goods, legal or not, then no one makes money.

So this is my play. I'll squeeze them until they serve Sanchez and O'Doyle to me on a fucking silver platter.

Those two bastards interfered in my business. They tried to take what's mine. To manipulate me. They killed my wife's brother. Set her apartment on fire.

I think of how Anna looked the first time she came to me. She was willing to pay her brother's debts with her body, and yeah, I let her.

I manipulated the whole thing just so I could have her.

I should regret it. I should feel bad, or something. But I don't.

Anna belongs to me, and I was going to have her any way I could get her.

The fact someone else tried to get to her pisses me off. That Sanchez thought he could hurt the woman I love, even if he didn't know she was mine, fills me with rage.

I think of how O'Doyle kept dicking around with me. Flaunting his daughter. Acting like we could maybe make some sort of alliance if I dumped my wife and married that simpering conceited child of his.

And I get mad.

Motherfuckers.

Dead motherfuckers. Both of them.

I sit in my office with my thoughts and my rage, and I think about my unborn child, and something else hits me.

Pride. And then fear.

Yeah, I was afraid when I got the call about Anna

being taken to the hospital. For the first time in my life, I care about something, about someone, more than I do myself.

Suddenly, I realize being afraid doesn't make me a coward. It makes me human, and that's something I was beginning to doubt.

My humanity.

But I am human. Very human. I was alone before, but I am not now.

Anna is my family. She's at home, growing our baby. Doing it for me. Cause she loves me, and my heart squeezes in my chest.

I'm going to be worthy of her. I will work every day to prove my worth.

If I have to hunt down every piece of shit threat to my organization and break their necks with my bare hands to keep her safe, I will.

But I don't think I'll have to. I think squeezing the others, letting them know who's the real king of this city will work for me.

It's not about who works harder, it's about who works smarter. And I don't need a degree to run this town.

No. They'll find Sanchez, and they will bring him to me. Because it's the only way I'll allow them to get back to business as usual in my fucking town.

And make no mistake, this is *my* fucking town.

I own it. And I run it.

If they didn't know that before, they do now. You don't walk into a viper's lair and fuck with him.

Not unless you want to die. And I got no problem with killing.

CHAPTER THIRTY-THREE-ANNA

Something snaps. A balloon or something. I twitch and I struggle to sit up in bed.

My eyes dart to the alarm clock and I see it's not even daylight yet. I feel groggy and out of sorts, but then my stomach cramps and I clutch it. I wince as a shudder rolls through me.

Then I feel it.

Wetness all around me, pooling between my legs.

"Nico?" I turn my head to my husband who's sprawled out on his belly. I shake his shoulder.

"Huh? Anna, you okay?" he says, and I can tell he is fully awake with just a moment's notice.

Fear and excitement fill me. Tears prick my eyes, and I bite my lip. Then I tell him.

"I think my water broke."

I t's still too early. Three weeks till my due date, but this baby is so big, I guess he needed more room or something.

Nico didn't even skip a beat when I woke him with the news. I'm so busy counting minutes between contractions I hardly notice him carrying me outside to the SUV and holding me the whole way to the hospital.

We know the birth will be difficult because wide hips or not, my husband is a huge man and our baby takes after him.

"We don't have a name," I say, looking at Nico as the panic of what's about to happen settles in.

"What name do you like?" he asks, holding my hand after he's placed me on a gurney.

I expect the hospital to tell him he has to wait somewhere else or something. But they don't. They simply push me to a private room where I see a dozen men in black standing in the hallway.

Security guards?

Angel is one of them, and he gives me a slight smile as he nods his head at Nico.

"Rosebud," Nico says, catching my attention. "Have you thought about names?"

He repeats his question and I try to think, but I'm having another contraction.

I feel sweat beading on my forehead, and I groan as my entire body feels like it's being squeezed between two vise grips.

Any conversation halts right then. My whole world is tilted as I'm being transferred from the gurney to a hospital birthing bed.

I've talked with both the doctor and Nico about wanting to try to give birth naturally, but I'm afraid. It hurts so much. And I must say something about it because suddenly Nico is there.

The nurses already lowered the front of the bed and raised the support bar, and I'm using it to lean on as the next contraction hits.

I feel my husband's powerful arms wrap around me, offering me even more support. He's saying things, wonderful things, in my ear. And he is kneeling on the bed behind me.

"You'll ruin your suit," I whimper inanely.

"I can get a new suit," he says, and I can hear the smile in his voice.

"Oh God, it hurts. I can't," I cry.

I feel my energy waning. I don't know how long it's been, and I'm tiring out. I wonder if it's too late for the epidural and I scream as another contraction rips through me.

But then Nico is there. His hands are holding me, soothing me, offering me comfort, and I take it. I grab onto him instead of the support bar, and it's like I can feel his energy pouring into me.

"Yes, you can, Rosebud. You can do anything."

"It's too hard," I whimper, still doubting myself.

And I hate that I feel that way. That I don't think I am strong enough. I've got a million fears and doubts all clawing at me, and I don't want to give into them. But it's hard to block them all out.

What if I mess up?

What if I am not any good at motherhood?

I hardly remember my mother, and the rest of my family, well, they were hardly there for me. I worry that Nico isn't going to take to fatherhood.

What if he gets tired of me?

What if having a baby is too much pressure on a guy like him?

I have so many worries. So many things I am afraid of. Some are more shallow than others, and I am ashamed that I even have them.

I shouldn't care about what Nico will think of my body after pregnancy. Or if he will ever find me sexy again after this.

But I do care.

Still, I can't voice any of that. If I do, I might break. So instead I focus on the now. On the pain of labor, that's breaking me in two.

"You're doing so good. You're so brave. Come on, Baby. I got you, Rosebud," he says right into my ear.

And he's right. He does have me.

"Okay, you are fully dilated, Mrs. Fury." The doctor turns and says something to the nurse, then she nods at me.

"It's time to push."

Hours later, I am exhausted.

Giving birth is just as hard as everyone says it is. But afterwards, well, afterwards there is this rush of emotion.

The doctor says it's hormones, but whatever it is I can't help but feel joyful.

The sounds of a squalling infant reach my ears and I smile tiredly.

"Is he okay?" I ask, and Nico tenses.

The puke green walls of the hospital room blur as I try to catch my breath. I've collapsed backwards onto my husband, who spent the entire process on the bed with me, arms around me as I delivered our healthy baby boy.

"You did so good, Rosebud. So good," Nico whispers, and he's kissing my temple.

I listen to the doctor who is still at the foot of the dropped bed. She's telling me to push, and I deliver the afterbirth, which is exactly what it sounds like.

I am almost embarrassed that my hot as fuck husband is here to witness all this, but really, I am too tired to deal with that feeling.

The nurses and neonatal care team are checking the baby, running him through APGAR tests, and weighing him. They even have this little baby alarm they clip to his umbilical cord after Nico cuts it, of course.

I guess that's so they can track him or make sure there aren't any *we accidentally switched your baby* mistakes.

Oh my God. Can you imagine that?

The idea makes me shudder in horror, and Nico's

arms tighten around me. He's still on the bed, and he's sitting behind me, his big thighs are cradling me between them, and he must be soaked sitting in all this mess, but I can't think about that now.

"Where is he? I want him," I say.

"He's coming," Nico answers.

Seconds later, a nurse places the most beautiful thing I have ever seen in my arms. He's so small and pink and his face is all squished. But he's so amazing.

Our son. We have a son.

"Look what you did, Rosebud. Look what you made. He's so perfect," Nico whispers, and I swear I hear tears in his voice.

His head is next to mine, his cheek brushing my skin, and I lean into him, tears filling my gaze as I look down at our little miracle.

"What do you want to call him?" my husband asks.

"Can we, I mean, would it be okay if his middle name is Samuel? My brother wasn't a good guy, I know, but he was named after our grandfather, and he was a good man. Maybe this will be like giving him a second chance," I whisper, wondering if Nico will understand or if he will hate the idea.

"Sure. Samuel, it is, but what about his first

name?" my husband asks, and my heart just about explodes with love for him.

"That's easy. His first name is Nico. Like his father," I say, and I feel my husband's shock as his whole body goes stiff.

He gently lifts up, turning my shoulders so I can look at him. God, I love this man.

"Yeah? You would name him after me?"

"Of course, he should have a good strong name, don't you think?"

"Yeah, yeah," Nico says and nods, palming the back of my neck with one hand and dropping a kiss on my forehead before he places his other hand on the baby.

"He's hungry," he says, smiling and I grin, lifting him to my breast for his first feeding.

"Welcome to the world, Nico Samuel Fury," he whispers, and I feel so full right then.

Full of love. Full of hope and happiness.

Trying to reconcile my new titles is surprisingly not difficult for me. I thought it would be. But it isn't.

I'm a father.

A husband.

The CEO of Viper Enterprises.

Owner of the Vipers' Den.

And king of the crime syndicate known as the Vipers.

I listen intently as I leave the condo. I don't want to wake Anna or the baby.

It's been six weeks since we brought him home, but I know he's still adapting to life outside the comfort of his mother's protective womb.

Six weeks.

It's important. The time I mean.

Yes, it has been longer than that since I've fucked my sweet wife. But six weeks was the number I've been counting down.

My body fucking vibrates with anticipation, but I press down on my growing cock unobtrusively before I flick my gaze to the guard.

He nods and I continue to walk to the elevator. Pride fills me and complete fucking devotion as I picture my wife, my brave beautiful Anna.

Six weeks.

The doc is coming over today to check on her. And, if all is good like it should be, then Anna and I can be intimate with each other.

I expect the doctor's report around six, and I can't fucking wait to get the all clear.

Yes, I know it's intrusive and heavy-handed to have Anna's doctor report to me. But I don't give a fuck. I need to know everything about my wife.

It's the only way I can bring myself to leave her side for a fucking second.

Six weeks.

Christ. I almost moan aloud at the thought of sinking into my wife's sweet sex.

Six weeks is a long time to abstain, especially with the feelings I have for this woman. and it's been longer with the bedrest.

No problem, of course, since obviously she was growing our child and then healing after the miracle of bringing our baby into the world.

My heart swells with love and pride and it is all for her.

My Anna.

My sweet Rosebud.

There isn't anything I wouldn't do for her.

The woman has me on my knees. But she's so goddamn cute she doesn't even seem to notice.

I would burn cities to the ground for her.

I know it's nuts. But I can't help it. She is precious to me.

I covet her. I need her safe. I want her happy. And with me. All the time.

I have big plans for tonight.

She is the best thing that ever happened to me and she deserves so much.

A big house.

A good life.

Safety.

Security.

And I am going to give it all to her.

I've already sent all my requirements to the realtor, and he already has some properties to show me.

"Boss," Angel says, walking into my office.

"What?"

"Someone's out front to see you," he says, and his face looks grim.

"Who?"

"Margaret O'Doyle."

Fuck.

I run a hand over my face. I don't want to deal with this. Margaret O'Doyle is fucking trouble, but I can't just walk away from my responsibilities.

I have to take this meeting.

CHAPTER THIRTY-SIX-ANNA

Mrs. Pirillo is sitting in the nursery where the baby is sleeping while I shower and dress.

I've never done this. Just surprised Nico at the Den. But I can't wait to see him tonight.

The doctor says I'm completely healthy and everything looks great, which, considering where she was looking, sounds kind of weird. But I am okay with it.

One thing no one talks about after you give birth is how every nurse and doctor on call in the hospital seems to stop by your room to check on your vagina.

Of course, when your husband is Nico Fury, that means all the staff are female and married.

After a while, you kind of get numb to it. Besides,

there is only one person I want face to face with my coochie. And that's my hot as fuck husband.

After six weeks of wearing functional, practical clothes. I want to look pretty. No more weird mesh underwear and enormous diaper pads. No more tops stained with breastmilk and ointment to keep the skin of my nipples from cracking.

I want to feel like a woman. I want Nico to look at me again with desire.

So, I dress carefully.

I was chubby before I was pregnant, so overall I did not gain a lot of weight. All the swelling at the end of my last trimester had something to do with retaining fluids. But that all went away within the first few days after I gave birth.

My boobs are definitely bigger, a side effect of breastfeeding. And I can't say I am not happy with how they look, because my cleavage is better than ever.

My stomach is soft and round, but that isn't new. I was always bigger, curvier. But Nico never seemed to mind before. And I am hoping he doesn't mind now.

I turn in the mirror and bite my lip. I am wearing a wrap dress with a flower print, perfect for a summer evening. It hugs my breasts and cinches at my waist, but the skirt is loose and swirls around my hips, landing above my knees in a flutter of soft fabric.

Sliding my feet into a pair of wedge sandals, I scrunch my curls and apply another coat of sheer lip gloss. I give Mrs. Pirillo a few last minute instructions and inform her I just pumped and put the milk in the fridge with the others.

I kiss my son, then I walk to the living room to wait for my ride. The intercom buzzes by the front door, and I go to answer it.

"Maria is here for you, Mrs. Fury," the guard sounds hesitant, but both Maria and Giselle are on their list of approved visitors.

"Okay, I'm coming out," I tell him.

It doesn't take long to convince the security guard that Nico is expecting me, and he calls for one of the cars to meet me downstairs.

"You look great," Maria tells me.

My smile turns into a frown when I notice her hesitancy.

"What's wrong? I'm sorry if me asking you to come with me is last minute—"

"Not at all, my shift starts in a half hour. So, this is perfect."

I nod, accepting her word.

"You're fidgeting."

"I'm nervous. I mean, it's one thing for a guy to be all hot and bothered about you before he witnesses your vagina splitting in two in a hospital room, but after?"

"Splits in two?"

"Have you ever seen someone give birth? It is not pretty. No one told me there would be so many fluids," I say, and I'm starting to breathe funny.

I think it's my nerves making me panic.

"Fluids?" Maria scoffs.

"Uh, yeah. First, your water breaks. Then there is blood and more amniotic fluid. And last, the afterbirth, which is every bit as horror movie worthy as it sounds," I tell her, and might actually be full on panicking at that moment.

"Then, because your baby is a giant, they have to repair your now broken vajayjay with sutures. I am talking real fucking stitches, Maria. I mean is he even going to want to touch me down there again, much less kiss me!"

My eyes are wide, and I slap a hand over my mouth. I can't believe I just said that. And Maria looks like she can't either.

We get inside the SUV. We buckle up and I tell

the driver where to go. Then I chance a glance at her face.

"Okay, wow. So, that was graphic," Maria says. "Um, how big was Baby Nico?"

"Ten pounds, six ounces and twenty-four inches long."

"Holy fuck."

"Yeah, No shit," I say.

"Well, I'm not gonna lie. Your baby is aggressively cute, and whenever I see him, I have serious cuteness aggression."

"Cuteness aggression?"

"Yeah," she says, "I just wanna bite him. I mean, I won't, but I don't know how you can stand it. He's just, ahh, so beautiful."

Pride fills me.

"You're right. The baby is perfect. And I confess I do kiss and nibble him all the time."

"Lucky heifer. But I bet Papa Nico feels that way about you."

"You mean he has cuteness aggression towards me?"

"Well, we'll find out when he sees you tonight with your big milk bags hanging out like that," she says.

"Milk bags?" I repeat, then I snort.

Then we both start giggling.

And the giggle grows.

And grows.

Until we are snorting with full on belly laughter.

The driver stops in the back of the Den, and I turn to Maria, my heart pounding inside my chest.

"I hope you're right."

"One way to find out," she replies with a shrug.

And I open the door.

"Well, nice place you have here."

Margaret O'Doyle is sitting at the bar in a red miniskirt and barely there halter top. She looks like something someone could buy, and maybe that's the point.

But I'm not buying. I'm not even looking.

"What are you doing here?"

"Can't a girl just stop in to say hi to her betrothed?"

I don't bother to sit. It's early yet and only a few regulars are inside the bar, imbibing their cocktails and letting loose.

The Vipers' Den is a popular hangout. It's Friday night, so I know we will be packed.

It isn't a place just for my guys, but for locals and

people looking for a Manhattan vibe in a Jersey City bar. The Den is dark with a sleek city theme, all iron, steel, and cement.

It's clean too. No drugs. No whores. No fights. Nothing obvious, anyway. Nothing that would make any hotshot cops curious.

I don't need that kind of aggravation.

I prefer to conduct business in my office below, but this woman is not an associate. She's nothing to me at all. And my patience is wearing thin.

"I'm a married man, Miss O'Doyle. And you and me, we're nothing."

"Oh please, your marriage is just a nuisance. A pittance that can go away with a simple signing of papers. We can have something good. I can fit in here," she says, and she is eyeing me like a spider eyes its dinner.

Repulsion fills me and I let her see it. She shrinks back.

"Nico, my f-father is gonna cut me off. And worse. He's gonna sell me to some old as dirt business associate and send me to live in some Eastern European country I can't even pronounce if I don't come back and tell him you said okay to this," she begs, and I see something I want to ignore.

I see fear.

Fuck.

CHAPTER THIRTY-EIGHT-ANNA

I don't recognize the security guards standing outside the Vipers' Den. But I haven't met all of my husband's people yet.

They must know Maria, cause they greet her and let us in.

I've been married to Nico for months, but I've only ever been in the Den twice. I don't know who he's told about me, or what anyone knows about me.

Suddenly, I feel foolish. Maybe surprising him isn't such a good idea.

"What are you waiting for?" Maria smiles.

"Come on," she says, tugging my arm.

But I feel sluggish and insecure. A sinking feeling is dragging me down, and it starts in the pit of my stomach.

I look for Nico among the scattered people. But first, I see Angel. He sees me, too.

Angel looks at me and his eyes go wide. He looks shocked. Like *oh shit* surprised.

It is not the kind of expression you make when you are happy to see someone. And that's weird.

He starts to head my way, but before my husband's cousin can reach me, I see him.

I see Nico, and a heavy weight lands right on my chest.

He's standing with his elbow on the bar, his body angled towards someone, and he is leaning down.

I guess he is trying to hear what the other person is saying over the thumping bass of the music.

It is always so loud in here.

Then he straightens his back, and I see who he is talking to. It's a woman. She's pretty and young.

Really pretty and young.

And she's looking at my man like the sun rises and sets on him. I take her in and pain begins deep in my soul.

She's super thin and fit, like she spends all day exercising and tanning. She's a knockout in a skimpy little getup and my mouth goes dry.

She is just the type of woman I could just imagine belonged with a man like Nico. And my heart cracks.

"Anna," Angel starts.

His hands are up like he's going to come between me and my destination. But I shake my head as a new emotion fills me.

Rage.

I take a step towards my husband.

Dirty. Lying. Cheating. Bastard.

Fury is his name, but he gave that name to me, and it is just so damn perfect for how I feel.

He looks so damn good. And it makes me even madder. My dark avenging angel of a husband is smiling at this stranger, and I want to scratch her eyes out.

And his. Mostly his.

The bass is really pounding now, or maybe that's my heart as I stride across the floor. I've never felt like this.

Possessive and furious.

It's like some comic book version of myself has been conjured from the depths of the fifth level of Hell and this new alter ego is bent on wreaking vengeance on him.

This man who belongs to me.

Images of the first time I ever saw him flit through my brain. I think of how he looked. Like a warrior. Tattooed and tall, his muscles rippling as he commanded me to get on all fours.

Heat pools in my belly and I'm shocked to feel arousal mixed with hurt.

The way Nico came at me that night, he was, well, he was divine. And my soul sang for him.

My body opened up like a flower at the slightest touch from his hands, and when he claimed me with his thick, heavy cock, I felt a freedom I had only ever dreamed of.

It scared me. So much so, I ran. But when I came back, when I needed protection, he gave it. He gave me his name. Took me to his home. Made me his.

He said he loved me.

Seeing him smile at this other woman is like a knife to my heart. The truth is so clear.

Nico is no angel come to take me to heaven.

He's a snake.

A serpent slithering in the grass, just lying in wait. Like the one who tricked Eve into biting that goddamn apple.

I'm close now.

There are only a few feet separating us, but this woman has his attention, and he doesn't seem to know I am there.

"—it's why I came to Boston. I promise I'll keep you

safe. You're my—what is it?" Nico says when her eyes look past him, landing on me.

He turns, and his blue eyes startle. He straightens his shoulders and his gaze rakes over me from head to toe.

"Guess I took the viper by surprise. I didn't think that was possible," I whisper, and my voice trembles.

"Anna—"

He moves like he's going to touch me. But bile fills my throat at the thought of his hands on me after he's touched her and I flinch, stopping him in his tracks.

I want to shout at him. To tell him to fuck off and drop dead. But I can't speak, so I pivot on my heels, turning my back on him.

I bump into some man, and the idiot thinks it's an invitation. He puts his hands on me, and I push against his chest.

"Where you going, Baby?" the stranger says right against my face, and the stink of alcohol makes me gag.

"Get the fuck off my wife!"

I hear Nico's voice boom right behind me right before the asshole is pulled off me. This man must not know my husband, because he's smiling at him with a smart ass reply.

Nico doesn't hesitate. He just reacts. With one punch, he sends the man flying across the room.

My stomach twists. It's some sort of sicko reaction to violence, I guess, because even though I am mad at him, it turns me on to see Nico defend me.

I'm so fucked up.

Chaos erupts. People start shoving and fighting. I know Nico is the boss. He shouldn't be doing this so publicly.

I watch for a moment and see him pummel that guy's face, his blue eyes blazing with vengeance.

Someone is yelling. Then Nico's guys are there. I watch Angel pull my husband off the man. Then I turn around.

They can handle it. I just need to get away.

"Anna!" I hear him call my name again, but I am too lost in my own hurt to slow down.

"Anna, are you okay?" Maria shouts as I push past her and Angel.

I ignore her, too. I can't look at her. I've been such a goddamn fool. Hot, angry tears roll down my face, but I don't bother wiping them. I jog down the stairs, to the hallway I'm so fucking familiar with.

I need to get to the alley. To the car. Back to the condo. To our son. And once I get there, I have to pack.

I'm not stupid enough to think I can get away from Nico with his baby, but I won't sleep in his bed.

Not now.

Not anymore.

Never again.

A sob wracks my body, and I stomp my feet and let out a short scream before grabbing the handle to the door leading to the alley.

That's when a body slams into me from behind, and the air whooshes out of my lungs.

"Where do you think you're going, Wife?"

CHAPTER THIRTY-NINE-NICO

I'm just closing the deal I made with the young O'Doyle when my world turns to shit.

I can't pinpoint how or why I didn't know it was about to happen.

Maybe my senses have dulled.

Maybe that's what being happy did to you.

Cause I am happy, I realize.

It's an alien feeling.

A strange one, but I want it.

I crave it.

I need it.

This young woman has big plans to oust her father's old world regime. I have to say, I'm shocked, but not surprised.

A lot of old time mafiosos are having difficulty

coming to terms with this new world we live in. Margaret O'Doyle wants to take her family into the 21st Century. And I approve.

It only takes me ten seconds to convince her she doesn't need to offer to spread her legs to do that. Relief shows on her face, and I'm glad.

She's pretty. But she's a baby. And I'm spoken for.

So, I offer a different deal. She gets rid of her father however she wants, tells me what she knows about Sanchez, and I will grant her the protection of the Vipers.

Plus, I'll open the gates back up.

The O'Doyle's make most of their bread running guns, but without access to the ports, that dries up their business.

I'm just summarizing our deal when I feel the hair on the back of my neck tingle. Margaret's eyes flick behind me and I turn.

At first, I can't tell what I'm looking at.

I mean, it's Anna.

I know it's Anna.

But holy fucking shit.

Where the hell did she get that outfit? It's not that I want her to change. I don't.

I just don't want her here wearing that.

Don't get me wrong, my wife is always beautiful.

But tonight she's all glitter and gauze.

She's a knockout.

I want to shout at everyone to leave the Den. I want to gut every motherfucker with eyes who can see her like this.

All that soft skin on display, all her sweet curves and delicious valleys, those are mine. And I am a greedy, jealous prick.

She belongs to me and me alone.

My little Rosebud is all wrapped up like a present in a flirty little dress that shows way too much of her gorgeous tits and those thick, tanned legs I've been dreaming of having wrapped around me.

I'll blame my slowness on the fact all my oxygenated blood has just rushed to my straining cock. That's why I don't register her anger and her hurt. Not before it's almost too late.

Anna turns her back on me, and it's like a punch to the stomach. I can't breathe. She's walking away. I can't move.

Then she's running, and so am I.

She's going downstairs, and I wonder if she means to go to my office. But then I know she's heading for the alley where I keep my cars waiting.

"Anna!" I yell for the second or third time, I don't know.

I hear Angel, maybe Maria, too, calling our names. But I ignore them.

I have to catch my wife before she gets out that door.

And when I do, I am going to show her what it means to turn your back on a viper.

CHAPTER FORTY-ANNA

"*Where do you think you're going, Wife?*"

Nico flexes his hips, and I cease my struggling. The thick bar of his cock is right against the crack of my ass. He flexes again and I bite my tongue to keep from moaning.

I don't want to like how it feels, but I do.

"Let me go," I tell him.

"No," he says then backs up, the steel band of his arms tight around my waist.

He picks me up, and I ignore the men standing guard outside his office. He dips his chin, and one opens the office door. Then we're inside and Nico kicks it shut.

He is still holding me when he slams one hand on the biometric pad, engaging all locks.

"Nico, I want to leave."

"Too bad," he says, bringing me to the bedroom I know is behind the second door.

I struggle.

How many other women has he had there?

"None. You are the only woman I have ever brought here. The only woman who ever slept in my bed at the condo. The only woman in my life, period."

I growl in frustration and stomp my foot down on top of his. Finally, he lets go, and I try to move, but he's blocking the way.

"Oh really? Then what was that upstairs, huh? You just giving out free protection to every girl in a tight dress?" I spit the question.

My chest is heaving, and his eyes are drawn to it. I want to kick him, but there's no room.

"Speaking of tight dresses," he growls, and his fingers dip between my cleavage as he pulls me closer.

My whole body is tingling. I shouldn't let him do this, but when he dips his head and claims my lips, I can't help myself. I kiss him back.

"You look so fucking good, Rosebud. You wear this for me?" he asks, and I feel his hand snake up my spine, gripping the base of my neck.

He tilts my head to deepen the kiss, and I let him. God help me, I participate. My tongue is sliding against his and I drink him in. His spicy sweet essence hits me hard, and I am drunk on it.

Then I remember the skinny woman upstairs and I bite down on his lower lip.

Hard.

Hard enough to draw blood.

Nico lifts his head. His eyes are blazing, and red stains his lips. But he's not mad.

I should have remembered this is Nico. He's no stranger to violence, and I think it turns him on even more.

"Feel this, Rosebud?" he asks, pressing his hard length against my belly before shoving my back onto the mattress.

"This is all for you."

"I don't want it," I lie.

"Yes, you do. You fucking love it. You love me."

His smile mocks me, and in that moment, I hate him.

"Nah. You got too much love inside that hot little body and your big heart, you might want to hate me. But you can't," he says, and it's true.

His hands slide up my thighs, lifting the skirt to

my dress, and Nico groans, his eyes on the lacy little thing I wore just for him.

"Fuck. You went outside like this?" he asks and grits his teeth.

Then he pulls my panties off, and I hear the lace tearing.

And the sound of that is hot.

So damn hot.

My pussy clenches, and proof of my arousal starts dripping down my thighs. This need I feel is deep, like soul deep. Something inside me is starving for him.

Like I've been incomplete without him. I'm still mad, but I want him.

"You wet for me, Rosebud? Let me see. Show your husband how hot you are for my dick," he grunts, pressing his enormous hands against my knees and forcing my legs to open wide.

"Godfuckingdamn. You're glistening," he says, and heat burns my cheeks.

But I can't be embarrassed. Not in front of this man who's seen me at my absolute worst.

"What about her?" I say as he starts to undo his pants with one hand.

"Her who?"

"Your little girlfriend upstairs," I grunt and try to shake his hold off me,

"What? Anna, there is no girlfriend. There is no one. There. Is. Only. You."

Nico's voice drops an octave, and he plunges all of his length into me with one hard push as he utters that last word.

He seats himself fully, his head drops back and pure bliss flutters across his face.

My mouth drops open. So many feelings fill me.
I'm confused.
I'm hurt.
I'm relieved.
I'm so full.
My sex clamps down around him. Nico grunts. He feels so good. Then he's crawling over me, using his muscles to push me up the bed while he remains buried inside.

"Nico," I whine, needing more, needing him.

"I got you, Baby. I missed this body. It's been too long since I've been inside this sweet pussy."

I agree. And I cling to him. My hands are gripping his waist, then lowering to shove his pants down farther so I can squeeze his ass.

Nico is a beast. He's dominant and intense. His body seems made for me. And I love every bit of it.

"Love you, Rosebud, so fucking much," he says as he fucks me.

He tears at my pretty dress, but I don't give two shits. I need to feel all of him, too. And as he rips off his shirt and presses his chest to my swollen, aching breasts I moan aloud.

"Fuck. S'good," he says.

I nod and watch as he claims me with his body. His face is a story. And that story is so damn complex.

He looks like he's in the throes of something biblical. Something heart wrenching and soul breaking. I want to soothe him. To ease whatever he is feeling, but I feel it, too.

His hands are on my throat, and he squeezes, those electric eyes watching me for every expression following my movements hungrily like he can't wait to learn everything about me.

I let him. I give him complete control of my body, and he rewards me with another long stroke of his dick, grinding his pubis against my clit and sending torrents of ecstasy racing through me.

The way he makes me feel, I can't describe it. It just gets better every time. It's *more* every single time.

My pussy twitches and flutters, I am so ready to explode.

"Tell me," he commands.

"Gonna, oh fuck, Nico, I'm coming."

And he's right there with me.

CHAPTER FORTY-ONE-NICO

I glance at Anna in the back seat with me. She's wearing one of the spare button downs I keep in my office.

I have extra slacks in my office, but she looked at me like I was out of my fucking mind when I offered, and I didn't push her.

I'm a big guy and the shirt is long enough on her that she's decent. She looks good in my clothes.

Sexy and rumpled.

Like she's just been well-fucked, which she has.

She smells like me, too. Like my soap. And I like it.

I fucking like it a lot.

We took a fast shower, rinsing off the mess we made and whereas I could put back on my pants and slide into another shirt, her dress and panties were hopelessly ruined.

But she's being quiet now.

Too quiet.

I have to talk to her. I want to know what she's thinking, but I won't ask her. Not where Tommy can hear us.

Sure, my driver is discreet. He has to be to keep his fucking job.

But this is personal.

So, I wait until we're in the elevator. My nerves are stretched taut, like Odysseus' bow strings.

I feel tight. So fucking tight. And ready to bust a vein.

"You lied."

"I never lied to you, Anna," I say, and I'm fucking hurt.

"You did. You said you went away on business. You said you loved me, but you were with her. Making plans to be with her," she says, and it breaks my heart.

"That's not what that was," I tell her.

"I heard you. You said she was why you went to Boston. And how you're gonna keep her safe. So what's that mean? She's under your protection now."

"Anna, you don't understand."

"You're right," she snaps, anger flashing in her whiskey eyes, and fuck it soothes my heart to see her like that.

Sure, it's fucked up. But I would rather have a spitting mad wife than one who doesn't care.

"I heard you say *you're mine.* But if she's yours, what does that make me?" Anna asks, her voice cracks on a sob and I reach for her.

But she pulls back, and this time I flinch. Anna is right. I did say that. But it's not what she thinks.

I'm a second away from telling her, but the elevator doors open, and I refuse to put on a show for the goddamn staff.

My face is hard, showing no emotion. And I barely react when the guard greets us.

I put my hand on Anna's back, biting my inner cheek to stop from reacting to the way she tenses, and I open the door, herding my wife inside.

She goes straight to the nursery, and I let her.

Anna is a terrific mother. I know she loves our son, and she won't do anything stupid like try to take him, so I wait for her in our bedroom.

When forty minutes pass and she doesn't show, I seek her out and find her sleeping in the rocking chair in the nursery.

Mrs. Pirillo, who is acting as a nanny of sorts, is on the small day bed we have inside the nursery, and I see disapproval in her eyes before she averts her gaze.

I know she is just doing her job, and I kind of like the fact she's protective of my Anna. But no one has to protect my wife from me.

I am her protection. I am her shield against all the bad things in the world.

But I am also the one who keeps hurting her. And I have to stop. I need to do better.

The line I am trying so hard to keep between my wife and my business, it's not working. It's causing her pain. And I won't have that.

I take a peek at my son, kissing my fingers and pressing them to his sweet, soft head. Then I turn to my wife, and I inhale.

I pick her up in my arms and she stirs a little. But she doesn't wake up until I place her on our bedspread. The one she made with her own hands.

Then she sits up.

"What are you doing?"

"Bringing you to bed."

"I don't want sleep here," she says, standing up.

She's pissed. And if I thought what she is thinking, I'd be pissed too. But she's still wearing my shirt and smelling like my soap, and the temptation is too damn great to pass up.

I grab either side of the collar and I rip it open, revealing her soft, naked skin to my hungry gaze.

"Goddamn. You're so beautiful."

"Nico," her breath hitches, and she struggles, but I have the fabric pulled down to her elbows and she can't do anything but follow my lead when I pull her tight to my body.

I'm only wearing shorts, and everywhere she touches I ache.

"You're my wife, Anna. You sleep in my bed every night. Remember?"

It's a low blow, reminding her of the rules I set when we first got married. Before I ever told her I love her.

"I don't want to."

"Anna, what you heard, it's not what you think," I try to explain, but the feel of her against me has my mind all foggy.

"Sure, it's not."

"I swear, it's not."

"How do I know you're not lying?"

"Rosebud, I love you."

I think that will reassure her, but it doesn't. My wife shivers, her whole body trembles against me and the taste of her salty tears is on my tongue before I realize I'm kissing her face, trying to stem their flow.

"You told me you weren't merciful, but I didn't believe you. Is this what you meant?"

"What?" I have no idea what she means.

"Saying you love me and then going to another woman—"

"I didn't go to another woman. Anna, look at me."

I tug the shirt all the way off her, and I am shaking now, too, as I sit on the bed and drag her nude body onto my lap.

And I am shaking with anger.

"I don't have mercy in me because no one has ever shown me any. But understand this, what I am about to tell you is more than I have ever told anyone."

I take a deep breath and slide my hand to the back of her neck, forcing her eyes to stay on me, even though she made no move to look away.

And then I tell her.

I tell her everything.

Every. Single. Fucking. Thing.

I tell her every bad fucking thing I did in my whole life. I'm leaning back against the headboard, and she's watching me, listening, unmoving.

And I confess it all. I lay it out for her. I tell her the real monster she's married to.

I tell her how I knew her brother was a loser. How I knew he couldn't pay me back, but how I used him to manipulate her into my bed.

How I kept her there because I am selfish and greedy.

I tell her that what she overheard was me making a business deal with the person who is going to take over the O'Doyle family business. I tell her about Sanchez, and how we're still looking for him. And I tell her how I control the docks.

Every drug dealer, gunrunner, and anyone involved in illegal imports has to come through me. That's how I started making money, by using my muscle to control the waterfront from Newark to Jersey City.

I tell her about my legitimate business, and how there is very little difference between being a real estate mogul and a crime lord.

The good news is I can control what goes on in my territory. That means no fucking trafficking of any kind. And absolutely no crimes against children.

I explain that if I ever told her a lie, it was to keep her from knowing about the darkness inside me.

I tell her I've hurt people. That I've killed men. And that I would do it again.

I don't want to scare her. I need her to be with me. But she obviously needs to know all of me to do that.

I've never been a do it halfway kind of guy. With me, it's all or nothing.

So right there, in the dim lighting of our bedroom, which is so different from how it looked just a couple of months ago, thanks to my talented wife, I have the one conversation I never thought I would ever have.

But in order to have her complete submission I have to give her this. So afraid or not, I take the leap. I allow someone to see the real me for the first time in my fucked up life.

"That's the only act of mercy I ever made, Anna. Now, I'm asking you. Can you forgive me? Can you be with me, knowing all this?"

I finish talking, and I wait for her decision.

She's so close I can count the gold flecks in her whiskey-brown eyes, and I do. I count them while my Anna takes a moment.

She licks her lips.

"You're wrong," she whispers.

I don't know what she's talking about, so I wait for her to continue.

"You are the most merciful man I have ever met."

"What? No, I'm not. I'm probably the most selfish fucking man you ever met," I counter, shaking my head.

"Nico, you asked me to listen, and I did. I hear you, Husband. Now, I need you to hear me."

I freeze while Anna lifts her hands to my face and rearranges herself, so she is straddling my lap. My hands go to her hips.

I'm rock fucking hard, and her heated pussy is soaking my shorts. But I don't know what she's about to say, so I don't move.

"You're a good man, Nico Fury. You're strong, and proud, and merciful. You help those in need, some who don't deserve it. Yeah, you do things off book, but the world is an imperfect place. Laws are human creations and humans make mistakes. You do your best in this fucked up world. And I love you for it," she says.

My eyes close and I drop my forehead to hers. I shiver. My whole body is coiled tight.

"I love you, Nico."

She says it again. I feel her hands slide between

us, she lifts up onto her knees, and I feel her pulling the waistband of my shorts down.

"Fuck, Anna."

She wraps her hand around my cock and positions me at her entrance.

"I love you," she says it again, sinking down and taking me all the way inside her.

I'm lost. Lost in her heat. Her wet warmth. Lost in her words.

"I love you," she says it again.

She keeps on saying it as she rocks her hips and rocks my world.

Finally, I snap out of my reverie. I clutch at her, lifting her up and slamming her back down. My lips cover hers, and I run my hands up her sides, to her back, her neck, her hair.

I pull on it, catching her moan in my mouth while she bounces up and down. Her big tits squish against my chest and I fucking love them. Every curve and dimple, every inch of her, is sublime.

"I love you, too, Rosebud. And I'm gonna keep loving you until the last breath leaves my body."

We move and writhe, each of us desperate for each other. And when we explode, it's together and I feel it in the very bottom of my soul.

Anna settles inside me.

She is everywhere. She surrounds me, confounds me, astounds me, and I am so fucking hers.

Anna wrecks me.

She cracks my heart open, and she changes everything.

She makes it better.

EPILOGUE ONE-ANNA

"What's the little guy up to?" Giselle asks over the phone.

"Well, he's sitting up now and when he has tummy time, he's getting up on his knees like he might crawl," I tell her excitedly.

I'm kind of bummed my bestie isn't here to see him achieve his latest milestone. Just like I'm sad she isn't here to see the new house.

After Nico and I had a very long and thorough heart to heart a few months back, he told me his plans and showed me the pictures of this place.

He'd already made an offer, and I was so glad he did. It's perfect. The outside is all stucco and brick, and we're at the end of a cul de sac in a suburb right outside Jersey City.

We waited to move in until renovations were complete. Like our new recreational wing that features a gym and an indoor pool, complete with retractable ceiling.

"Did you paint? I like that color," Giselle says.

"Yeah. Isn't it pretty?"

I lift the phone so she can see the light blue walls we painted in Nico Jr.'s room.

We are calling the baby Jr. for short. I say my goodbyes and end the call, Jr. on my hip as I go to the kitchen.

Mrs. Pirillo decided to come with us to the suburbs, and she has a room now in the house. With her children all grown and she and her husband separated, it was kind of ideal for her.

I'm glad. I love having her around. I'm not comfortable with the idea of a nanny just yet, but I do appreciate her watching the baby while I work on my sewing projects.

I hear the rumble of an engine pull up and excitement hums in my veins. It's Nico.

We go out to celebrate date night once a week, but he's early. I haven't showered or dressed yet, and the baby is still awake. He claps his hands when he sees his daddy coming.

I'm smiling so wide when Nico comes in, striding

right for me with a look of such intensity on his face I feel it to my toes.

"Wife," he moans, kissing me hello, then he turns his attention to our son.

"Hey little guy," he says, and gives Nico Jr. dozens of kisses on his cheeks and neck.

The baby reaches for him, and Nico scoops him up, continuing their love fest. I just smile and Mrs. Pirillo joins me.

"I never pictured him for a family man, but would you look at that? My oh my," she says, waggling her salt and pepper eyebrows.

I sigh and nod along, standing next to her.

Look at that, indeed.

My gorgeous husband is a complete cinnamon roll for our little boy, and I swear my ovaries are erupting like fireworks, desperate to give him more babies.

At least ten more.

I swear my pussy starts to protest, then she gets all warm and wet too, just looking at my big sexy husband making goo-goo faces.

"Here, I'll take him. This little man needs his dinner," Mrs. Pirillo approaches and reaches for the baby.

Nico hands him over, turning to me with his eyes

blazing blue fire. He takes my hand and leads me to our room.

Our bedroom is enormous. Twice the size of our old one with walk in closets and an ensuite bathroom that puts the one in the condo to shame. And that is saying something.

It's more luxurious than anything I ever saw. But it suits my husband. And it suits me.

"So, um, I haven't showered yet or anything," I say, and I'm running my hand over my head, a lame attempt to tidy myself as he closes our door and turns to face me.

His gaze is hungry. He licks his lips and stares at my yoga pants and tank top like I'm wearing something sexy.

"I like it when you're dirty, Wife," he says, pressing me against the wall.

His lips close over my carotid artery. He sucks, then Nico bites down and my pussy clenches.

"You do, huh? Show me," I say, my gaze half-lidded as I run my fingers up his neck and over his head.

"My pleasure, Wife."

Then he drops to his knees. And I shake my head and moan as he tugs my pants down over my hips.

It might be his pleasure, but it's definitely mine, too.

EPILOGUE TWO-NICO

E*arlier that evening*

Thunder roars in my ears as I rip off the crime scene tape surrounding my burned down warehouse.

We've got him. And I can't wait to exact my revenge.

"She deliver?" I ask, and Luc nods.

"Took some persuasion, but after her old man died of an *accidental overdose* and Margaret O'Doyle made the executive decision to out this piece of shit," Luc grunts.

I know he has a beef with the guy, too. Something having to do with Maria. But honestly, I don't care.

I'm too involved with my wife and son to keep up to date on the romantic entanglements of my men.

I turn my gaze to Sanchez, and that asshole is mumbling behind the duct tape sealing his mouth shut.

"Yeah, I can't hear you pal," I tell him, and really I'm not interested.

"You fucked with the wrong man," I say, then I get close, real close.

So close, I can smell the piss soaking his jeans.

Gross.

"I could have forgiven you for coming after my business. But you made this personal when you tried to hurt my wife."

I rip the tape off.

"S-she wasn't your wife then, man!" Sanchez says, like that fucking matters.

He doesn't get it. He doesn't understand.

Anna has always been mine.

Since the beginning of fucking time.

Every bit of her belongs to me. Her past, her present, her future. Her pain, her happiness. Her pleasure, and her agony.

All mine.

I inhale and breathe in his stink before I push the

blade into his gut. Then I drag it up, fileting the rotund motherfucker like a codfish.

I step back and away from the mess he makes, and I toss the knife to Luc, who catches it by the handle.

"See to it this gets cleaned up."

And I leave.

I have a date with my wife, and I can't wait to get home.

"I can't believe you did this," Anna says as we soak in the hot tub in our bathroom.

I'm deliciously sated after feasting on my wife's sweet pussy, before filling her with my dick until I could watch the cum dripping out of her, so it takes me a moment to realize what she's talking about.

"The tattoo?" I ask and glance down.

It's a blooming rose with a serpent wrapped around it and another vine stemming from it with a single bud. It's our family. She's my Rosebud and I'm the viper lying in wait beneath her leaves.

I'll fucking destroy any threat to her and my son,

and any other children we have. They're mine. Mine to love and to protect.

"Did it hurt?" she asks.

"Nah. If it did, it doesn't matter. I'd do it again to show you how much I love you," I say, kissing her temple.

"Silly man, I never want you hurt," she says, but I know she likes the new ink. She can't stop tracing it with her soft fingertips.

"I'd do it again, Baby. However many times it takes. I'd do anything for you. Rip my chest right open and hand you my heart if you want it. If it means you'll believe me," I tell her honestly.

"Why do you say things like that to me?" she asks, her throat working to swallow her emotion.

"You know why."

"Nico, Nico, Nico," she repeats my name like a litany,

"You're mine now, Rosebud. I'm keeping you forever."

"I'm yours. And you're mine," she says, and pure joy fills me.

"You're gonna stay right here with me, where you belong. Won't you, Baby?"

"Yes, Nico, oh yes."

I stand up and take her with me, water slides off

our skin. Carefully, I step out of the tub, making sure she doesn't slip.

"Good. Because I am nothing without you," I say, standing in front of the floor to ceiling mirror wall.

I should hand her a towel. But I don't. I like looking at her. Her soft body glitters with a million tiny drops of water, and it's like she's covered in diamonds.

"Christ, I love you, Nico." Her head tips back and her whiskey eyes smile as she bites her lip.

"Come here and show me, Wife," I say and pull her to me.

"Good Girl," I murmur as she slowly drops to her knees.

My sweet wife opens her mouth and takes me into her throat, and I'm done talking. I'm done thinking.

The only thing left for me to do is *feel*.

And, goddamn, do I feel fine.

T he end.

Did you enjoy Merciful Lies?

Please consider dropping a line or two in a review so other readers can enjoy it, too.

Want more Jersey Bad Boys Books?
Visit my website today:
https://www.cdgorri.com/series/jersey-bad-boys

**Available in paperback, hardcover, and with new discreet covers. Look for the audiobooks soon.*

Thank you and happy reading!
del mare alla stella,
C.D. Gorri

P.S. Indie authors like me count on word of mouth to get my books seen, so if you have a blog or a social media account and you want to post about my books, be sure to include #cdgorribooks so I can see it and I will share to too. THANK YOU.

These wild billionaire playboys are used to getting their way...

There isn't much money can't buy, especially when it comes to pleasure. But can these curvy women tame these billionaire beasts and win their love? Or will their souls be sucked into oblivion by the wanton bliss their bodies crave more and more with every surrender?

Each of our heroes wears a mask on the outside to face the world, but his disguise comes off when he runs into the one female who makes his blood run hot. Need and possessive passion abound in these books, but our heroes know only one way to control their desires.

Will they f*ck the feeling they see as weakness out of their systems, or will their needs only grow more wild with every touch, kiss, and plunge into ecstasy with the object of his affections?

Our Billionaire Heroes

Adrik Volkov
Marat Volkov
Josef Aziz
Andres Ramirez

Content Warnings

**This series has profanity, graphic, steamy scenes, violence, homicide, talk of deceased relatives, references to sexual assault and abuse (not by the MCs), mention of domestic violence (not perpetrated by MCs), mention of suicide, alcohol consumption, misogyny (not the MCs), questionable morals, hurtful past, manipulations, fake relationships, lies, revenge, forced marriages, very bad decisions, and romantic obsessions that may be unhealthy. The FMC works at a shelter for abused women and children.*

This is a fictional story with fictional characters. This is not real life.

*Always take care of your mental, emotional, and physical
self because you are important.*

P.S.

For those who asked Adrik is pronounced Ade-drick
and Marat is Meh-Rut. Happy reading!

WANT SHORT AND STEAMY ROMANCE?
TRY THE CHERRY ON TOP TALES!

Do you love spicy romance with sizzling encounters, insta love, and passionate romances you can read in a couple of hours?

Full steam contemporary romance short stories where love is just the cherry on top?

Then Cherry On Top Tales are for you!

Get your copy today. This series is so hot, you'll never want the stories to end.

Her Yule His Log
His Carrot Her Muffin
Her Chocolate His Bar
His Pickle Her Jam

The Falk Clan Tales:

The Bear Claw Tales:

The Barvale Clan Tales:

Barvale Holiday Tales:

Purely Paranormal Romance Books:

The Wardens of Terra:

The Maverick Pride Tales:

Dire Wolf Mates:

Wyvern Protection Unit:

Jersey Sure Shifters/EveL Worlds:

The Guardians of Chaos:

Twice Mated Tales

Hearts of Stone Series

Moongate Island Tales

Mated in Hope Falls

Speed Dating with the Denizens of the Underworld

Hungry Fur Love

Island Stripe Pride

NYC Shifter Tales

A Howlin' Good Fairytale Retelling

Witch Shifter Clan

Young Adult/Urban Fantasy Books

The Grazi Kelly Novel Series

The Angela Tanner Files

G'Witches Magical Mysteries Series

Co-written with P. Mattern

Witches of Westwood Academy

with Gina Kincade

Blackthorn Academy For Supernaturals

**Be sure to check out my BUY DIRECT BUNDLES and get 30% off when you buy available only my website.*

Click here for The Official C.D. Gorri Reading List - free download

Coming Soon

Motley Crewd Shifters

ABOUT THE AUTHOR

USA Today Bestselling author C.D. Gorri writes paranormal and contemporary romance and urban fantasy books with plenty of steam and humor.

Join her mailing list here: https://www.cdgorri.com/newsletter

An avid reader with a profound love for books and literature, she is usually found with a book in hand. C.D. lives in her home state, New Jersey, where many of her characters and stories are based. Her tales are fast-paced yet detailed with satisfying conclusions. If you enjoy powerful heroines and loyal heroes who face relatable problems in super-natural settings, journey into the Grazi Kelly Universe today.

You will find sassy, curvy heroines and sexy, love-driven heroes who find their HEAs between the pages.

Wolves, Bears, Dragons, Tigers, Witches, Vampires, and tons more Shifters and supernatural creatures dwell within her paranormal works. The most important thing is every mate in this universe is fated, loyal, and true lovers always get their happily-ever-afters.

In her contemporary works, you will find fiercely possessive men and the smart, confident, curvy women they are crazy about. As always, the HEA is between the pages.

Thank you and happy reading!
del mare alla stella,
C.D. Gorri

http://www.cdgorri.com
https://www.facebook.com/Cdgorribooks
https://www.bookbub.com/authors/c-d-gorri
https://twitter.com/cgor22
https://instagram.com/cdgorri/
https://www.goodreads.com/cdgorri
https://www.tiktok.com/@cdgorriauthor